No, Eddie thought. *It can't be!*

Looking up at the skylight, Eddie's eyes bulged in amazement. It couldn't be — but it was!

Eddie was on his feet so fast it made his head spin. He flung open the door and found Norby sound asleep with the teddy bear clutched in his arms.

Eddie screamed at Norby at the top of his lungs.

Norby popped up and hissed, "Shh! You'll wake the baby!"

"THE BABY'S ON THE ROOF!" Eddie cried.

A *novelization by*
RON FONTES *and* JUSTINE KORMAN

Based on the screenplay by JOHN HUGHES

Troll Associates

Special thanks to Laura Rubenstein and Laurens R. Schwartz

chapter 1

*O*ne fine and sunny day, Baby Boo's nanny, Henrietta, said, "Baby Boo, today you shall go on a wonderful adventure!"

Sixteen-month-old Bennington Austin Cotwell IV wriggled with pleasure as he heard the familiar words. Bennington was far too cute to be called by his full name. So everyone called the lively little boy Baby Bink.

At that moment, Baby Bink was snuggled in a soft, terry-cloth sleeper sitting on the knee of his pretty, young nanny, Gilbertine. Her crisp white apron smelled of laundry soap and starch. Her shiny, honey-blond hair smelled of shampoo.

Outside the Cotwell mansion, birds sang in the fresh, summer morning. Baby Bink greeted the day as he always did, by hearing Gilbertine read his favorite book. Baby Bink loved *Baby's Day Out.* He could listen to that storybook again and again and again! His chubby hand reached eagerly toward the book.

Gilbertine's green eyes drifted away from the page, but she knew the story by heart, so she continued, "You will see the many, many sights of the big city." Gilbertine stopped reading and sighed. "Couldn't we read another book?" she asked. "We've read this one a hundred times."

Baby Bink shook his blond head and pointed to the well-worn picture book. "Boo-boo! Boo-boo!" he cried. That's what he called his favorite book.

Gilbertine looked around the luxurious nursery. In one corner stood a tall, antique bookshelf. The shelf was filled with enough expensive picture books to start a small library.

"You have so many other books," Gilbertine said.

Baby Bink's chubby fingers curled into fists. His bottom lip puffed in a pout. "Boo-boo!" he cried. "Boo-boo!"

Gilbertine begged, "Pleeeease? Nanny Gilbertine is so tired of the boo-boo book, she could just gag."

Baby Bink slapped the book. "Boo-boo!"

Gilbertine smiled despite her frustration. She loved Baby Bink almost as much as if he were her own child. So Gilbertine continued the story. "After a lovely breakfast, Henrietta and Baby Boo left their fine house on Elm Avenue with its great chimneys and tall trees."

Baby Bink pointed to the picture in his beloved boo-boo. There was a fine, big house that looked a lot like the Cotwell mansion. At that very moment, Sally the maid was carrying up Baby Bink's delicious breakfast on a silver tray.

Baby Bink rested his head against Gilbertine's shoulder. He felt her voice rumble as she recited the next lines. "Henrietta and Baby Boo walked down the lane to the corner, where they boarded a big blue bus. They were on their way to the big city. Baby Boo felt very grown-up indeed, for this was his first trip away from Mother and Father."

Baby Bink smiled at Gilbertine. He had never gone away from his mother and father. But someday soon Bink hoped he would be grown-up like Baby Boo.

Sally tapped softly on the oak door, then let herself into the nursery. The short, round maid huffed from the long flight of stairs. Balanced carefully on the silver tray was a bottle of milk, a steaming bowl of oatmeal, and a sliced orange artfully arranged on a fine china plate.

Gilbertine gently lifted the boy off her lap and into his high chair. Bink sucked an orange slice while Gilbertine continued the story. "The big blue bus whooshed down the road. Under a bridge, over a hill, and into the big city it went."

Baby Bink bounced up and down in his chair. He was pretending he was riding in the big blue bus.

"Boo-boo!" Bink cried as he pointed to the picture of the big city.

While Gilbertine read on, Sally huffed up the stairs with a second silver tray. She carried this one to the sunny breakfast nook just off the mansion's master bedroom.

As usual, Sally found Laraine and Bennington Austin Cotwell III in their silk pajamas and robes, seated at the cozy table for two. Bing, as everyone called Mr. Cotwell, was reading the morning newspaper. He used a gold fountain pen to jot notes in the stock market columns. Bing was a trim, handsome man with a firm jaw and a fine head of dark hair.

Laraine smiled at Sally's punctual arrival and eagerly poured herself a cup of perfectly steeped, English breakfast tea. Sally poured Mr. Cotwell a cup of perfectly brewed coffee before silently taking her leave.

Laraine's perfectly groomed dark hair fell to just below her delicate jaw. Her clear ivory skin contrasted prettily with her dark eyes.

Laraine savored her first sip of tea. Then she said, "Did I tell you? The baby's having his picture taken this morning."

Bing sipped his coffee, then smiled at his perfect, young wife over the top of his newspaper. "Say hello to old Willy for me," Bing replied, burying his nose once more between the printed pages.

Laraine took another sip of her tea before gathering the courage to continue. "Willy isn't doing it."

Bing was such an old stick-in-the-mud when it came to tradition. Laraine worried about how he would react to her latest decision. "I've hired Downtown Baby Photographers," she said.

The newspaper slid down to reveal a handsome face that was an older version of Baby Bink's — right down to the pouting lower lip. "Old Willy's been photographing Cotwell babies since the Great Depression," Bing said. His deep, aristocratic voice took on just the hint of a whine.

Laraine took a deep breath, then launched into the arguments she'd prepared while brushing her hair earlier that morning. "Old Willy's a sweet soul and, in his way, he's a fine photographer. But his pictures are never published. The babies look like they're from another time."

Bing thought of his own baby pictures, in which he looked just like his father, who looked just like his grandfather, and so on down the long, comfortable line of Cotwells. "Exactly," he said with unashamed satisfaction.

Laraine struggled to keep the impatient edge out of her voice. "Willy hasn't had a photograph in the newspaper in twenty years."

"That long?" Bing asked. Time went by so quickly. One had meetings, golf, tennis, vacations, parties, more meetings, and on it went. Tiresome, really, most of it, and yet one bore up as best as one could — stiff upper lip and all that.

"Yes!" said Laraine.

Bing thought of the genteel, old photographer with his bow ties and liver-spotted hands. "Poor, old Willy."

Laraine's patience was at an end. Sometimes Bing just seemed to live in his own world. He was a dear, but he could sometimes be so insensitive.

13

"Poor old *us*!" she cried. "Everyone we know has had their baby's picture in the paper. Bink's over a year old and he's virtually unknown. I can't count the number of times I've been asked why we're keeping our baby a secret."

"That's just ruthless small talk," Bing replied.

"That doesn't make it hurt any less," Laraine said. It was her turn to pout.

Bing's blue eyes widened. At last the light had dawned. He nodded. "You're right. The only way to quiet that kind of talk is to have our friends open their newspapers and see a photograph of the prettiest baby in the city. Downtown Baby Photographers it is!"

But at that moment, Mr. Charlie of Downtown Baby Photographers was tied to a chair in an abandoned factory. Rough ropes pressed against his navy wool blazer. The embroidered patch on the breast pocket showed a smiling baby. But Mr. Charlie wasn't smiling. The frightened photographer was gagged.

Parked outside the factory, the Downtown Baby Photographers' van was painted with a big, smiling baby. Inside were Mr. Charlie's assistants in their fuzzy mohair sweaters. On the chest of each sweater was an embroidered smiling baby. But Mr. Charlie's assistants weren't smiling either. They were scared! Three thugs in black ski masks were inside the van too. They took the assistants' fuzzy sweaters and dumped the assistants out of the van.

Then, the leader of the thugs opened a black appointment book he'd found in the glove compartment. He read the list of appointments for that day. It said: COTWELL BABY. 3 COVENTRY LANE. 10:00 A.M. The man smiled an evil smile and slammed the book shut.

Meanwhile, at 3 Coventry Lane, Bennington Cotwell III was about to leave the mansion without saying good-bye to Bennington Cotwell IV.

Laraine stood in the mansion's marble entranceway and shook her finger playfully at her husband.

"What did you forget?" she scolded.

Bing patted the hand-sewn pocket of his summer-weight suit. "My pen!"

Mr. Andrews, the silver-haired butler, hastened to supply the gold fountain pen. Andrews had been in the Cotwell family for as long as Bing could remember, and he was far less absent-minded than his employer.

"What else?" Laraine persisted.

Bing felt just a bit peevish. "Darling, you know I hate to play games in the morning."

Laraine's perfectly manicured hands gestured to Baby Bink, who was balanced on Gilbertine's hip. Bing smiled. "Of course. How could I be so absent-minded?"

Bing hurried to the nanny.

"My pride! My joy! My son! My heir!" Bing punctuated each exclamation with a kiss on Baby Bink's smooth forehead.

Gilbertine inwardly flinched at each *my*. She remembered how unselfish her own parents had been and the many sacrifices they had gladly made for her and her brothers and sisters. Gilbertine fondly recalled the way her mother's eyes filled with tears whenever any of her children was hurt or sad.

The nanny knew that deep down her employers were good people and even good parents. But she couldn't help wondering if they ever saw Baby Bink just as Baby Bink. Sometimes, Gilbertine thought, he seemed to be nothing more to his parents than another possession — *my* car, *my* designer handbag, *my* baby.

Gilbertine was brought back to the present by Mr. Cotwell's fingers waving in Baby Bink's face. "Don't get into any mischief while Da-Da's gone," Bing cooed.

Once her husband was gone, Laraine faced the serious business of the day — how to dress Baby Bink for his photo session! Laraine stared at the tiny outfits filling a walk-in closet. Gilbertine tried to help with the selection.

Baby Bink sat in his playpen, turning the pages of his favorite book. Bink gurgled at the familiar picture of a big construction crane. He wished he could visit a work site, just like Baby Boo!

Laraine shook her head at the outfit Gilbertine held up for her approval. Normally she let Bink's nanny dress the baby. But today was much too important for that.

Laraine tried to explain the problem. "He has to look angelic. Like a little prince."

Gilbertine looked at the racks of fine clothes — velvet, corduroy, wool, and cotton. Only the best, and enough to keep a dozen children warm. Her mistress had said "a little prince," which reminded the nanny of *The Little Prince,* a book she had once tried to read to Baby Bink. But, like each book that wasn't *Baby's Day Out,* Bink had ignored it completely and cried for his "boo-boo."

The little prince in the book wore a blue coat down to his toes. "How about blue?" Gilbertine asked. She turned automatically at the sound of Bink's voice. He had turned the page and was looking at a picture of a pigeon. He gurgled with pleasure at the bird in his precious boo-boo.

"Blue?" Laraine asked. "Won't that be too obvious? Won't it look like we're trying to match his eyes?"

Gilbertine looked at Bink's mother and said, "I see lots of babies with blue eyes in blue outfits."

"What kind of babies?" Laraine demanded.

Gilbertine's forehead wrinkled. Sometimes she didn't understand Mrs. Cotwell at all.

Laraine's continued, "Pretty babies? Rich babies? Regular babies? Important babies?"

Gilbertine was not sure how to reply. "Regular babies," she answered softly.

"Baby Bink isn't a *regular* baby," Laraine said firmly.

chapter 2

*A*s the Downtown Baby Photographers' van rode out of the city, a rusty old van rumbled along behind it. Inside, the leader of the three thugs flipped through a tattered file of newspaper clippings. The leader's name was Eddie Mauser, and he was quite sure he was smarter than his younger companions-in-crime, Norby LeBlaw and Veeko Riley. But, unfortunately for Eddie, that wasn't saying much.

Eddie's dark eyes passed quickly over a photograph of Bing and Laraine at a gala fund-raising dinner. His eyes narrowed in greedy anticipation when they fell on the headline of an article from a leading financial magazine: "America's Richest Families." Other articles announced Baby Bink's birth and the building of the luxurious Cotwell Building in the city.

Eddie smirked with satisfaction as he reviewed an

article in a gardening magazine, which described in detailed prose and lavish photos the grounds of the Cotwell estate. Better still was the decorating magazine's spread featuring a tour of the Cotwell mansion, including a floor plan. Quite useful indeed!

The last article in the file was about the Downtown Baby Photographers — "the baby photographers to the rich and famous." *That's us!* Eddie thought smugly to himself.

By the time the Downtown Baby Photographers' van reached the Cotwell estate, Baby Bink had been washed, dried, powdered, combed, curled, and dressed in what Laraine had finally decided was the perfect outfit.

As the van pulled to a stop in front of the mansion, a low whistle escaped Eddie's lips. He pressed a false mustache onto his upper lip and adjusted a black beret over a flowing dark wig.

Though he had just seen dozens of photographs of the huge, elegant building, the sight of it in person took Eddie's breath away. *Did people really live like this?* Eddie wondered. His dark mustache lifted in a slow grin. *People do live like this,* the thug told himself. *And today is the day Eddie Mauser joins the upper class too!*

Eddie exited the van with grave dignity. His white-gloved hands tugged at the yellow tie and the lapels of the navy wool blazer he had taken off the real photographer. Eddie felt ridiculous, but it was all part of The

Plan. That's how Eddie thought of this scheme. Capital T, capital P. It was the heist of a lifetime. The big score. The pot of gold at the end of his personal rainbow.

Eddie recalled the photographer as they had left him in the factory, tied to a chair in his underwear. *What a chump!* Eddie thought. He couldn't imagine wearing this monkey suit day in and day out to snap pictures of rich babies. But for one day, one very special day, Eddie was willing to wear anything — even the silly eyeglasses and a starched white shirt.

Eddie watched his companions descend from the van and chuckled silently to himself. Eddie couldn't decide who looked more ridiculous — Norby or Veeko. Both young men wore the uniform of Downtown Baby Photographers assistants: white slacks and gloves, and a fuzzy mohair sweater embroidered with the smiling baby face logo.

Norby's powder-blue sweater hung loosely off his small, thin frame. A toothpick twitched from one side of Norby's mouth to the other. He peered at Eddie nervously through the rose-tinted sunglasses that were part of his disguise. Eddie wondered if Norby's beard looked too fake, then decided it would have to do. Norby had no class and there was just no way to hide that. Eddie shook his head and thought Norby and Veeko would be completely lost without him.

If possible, Veeko was even more brainless than Norby. But Eddie found Veeko's brute strength useful. Veeko looked ludicrous in the pink mohair sweater that barely stretched over his muscular chest. Veeko's blond flattop was hidden under a curly wig that reached his broad shoulders. A fake mustache drooped over his mouth, which hung open in awe at the sight of the mansion. A pink wad of gum teetered at the edge of his teeth.

"This is some *pied-à-terre,* huh?" Eddie demanded. He wasn't sure what the French expression meant, but he knew that a *pied-à-terre* was a place rich people owned and it sounded classy.

"Just excellent," Norby agreed.

Veeko resumed his gum chewing and said, "I bet they got a bathroom upstairs and downstairs."

Norby sighed. "Veeko, they got bathrooms *in* the bathrooms."

Veeko adjusted his white cap as he struggled to imagine what a bathroom in a bathroom would look like. He briefly wondered if Norby was teasing him.

"Get the gear," Eddie said impatiently.

While Veeko and Norby returned to the van, Eddie took a small note pad from his blazer pocket. He compared the rough diagram he'd drawn of the Cotwell mansion, including driveways, paths, and service roads, to the actual site.

Eddie was quite pleased with what he saw. Just as in the magazine, the mansion was surrounded by thick bushes and tall plants to capture the mood of an English garden. Eddie smiled to himself. Thank goodness rich people thought only of the way things looked to each other, not to an experienced thief. Far from an English garden, the leafy landscaping through Eddie's eyes meant plenty of easy places to hide near downstairs windows.

He flipped the notebook closed and pushed his shoulders back into a more dignified posture. With his pinkie extended in his best imitation of a lady holding a teacup, Eddie pressed the doorbell.

In seconds, the heavy oak door opened on an elderly gentleman wearing a fancy black suit and crisp white shirt. Eddie had never seen anyone so dignified, outside of the movies. "Good afternoon," the man said in a slow, deep voice.

Eddie grinned his most charming grin. He talked the way he thought a high-class baby photographer would sound. "A most pleasant and charming good day to you, sir. I'm Mr. Charlie."

Eddie tapped the smiling baby emblazoned on his jacket pocket. "Photographer *d'babe*, entirely at your service," Eddie added, thinking the touch of French was very classy indeed. Then he bowed, the way fancy folks did in the movies.

Eddie heard the man clear his throat. Then the slow, deep voice whispered, "I'm the butler, sir."

Eddie popped up from his bow. His face felt hot, but not just from bending over. All his fancy manners had been wasted on a servant! But Eddie quickly recovered his cool.

"Of course!" The butler. Didn't everyone have

butlers? Eddie wondered what butlers did, other than answer the door. To cover his confusion, Eddie turned to the van and snapped his fingers and called, "Time's wasting, gentlemen!"

Eddie turned back to the butler. "My assistants."

The man did not react at all. It was as if his features were carved in stone. Eddie tried to sound snooty and slightly offended. "You *were* expecting us?"

The statue nodded gravely, and Eddie found himself, Norby, and Veeko being led inside the elegant mansion. The entrance hall looked just as it had in the photographs. But nothing had prepared Eddie for the sound his shoes made on the black-and-white Italian marble floor or the sweet aroma that rose from a gigantic bouquet of fresh flowers clutched in a priceless antique vase.

Eddie had lived in apartments smaller than this entrance hall, but he struggled not to be intimidated by his awesome surroundings. *If all goes according to The Plan,* Eddie consoled himself, *someday I'll be living in a place like this!*

Mr. Andrews led the photographer and his assistants to the library, where all the Cotwell babies were photographed. Then Mr. Andrews left. The room was a symphony in subdued shades of blue and gold. A fine Oriental rug spread over a parquet floor. Blue bookshelves reached to the high ceiling. The massive, white fireplace was decorated with floral plasterwork and the Cotwell family crest. Comfortable chairs and ottomans flanked large sofas. Eddie had never been in such a room. It looked even more expensive than the outside — and that was saying a lot. Eddie liked expensive. *Hey, I could get used to this!* he thought.

Eddie took his eyes off the impressive decor when he heard Veeko's voice.

"Ed? May I . . ."

Eddie saw the young thug holding a heavy paper-weight. He gestured as if to put the silver object in his pocket.

Eddie glared. Idiots. He was working with small-time idiots! He scolded Veeko, "We ain't here to nick no bric-a-brac-a! We're here for the hit of a lifetime. You want to be a shoplifter, go to J.C. Penney."

"You really think we can pull this off?" Veeko asked.

Eddie snapped sarcastically, "No, I'm here 'cause I got a curiosity about the electric chair."

"What about the baby?" Veeko persisted nervously. "I don't know squat about babies."

Eddie sighed. Veeko always got jumpy just before a heist. "I'll tell you all you gotta know about babies. They're two-foot long and dumber than *you*."

Veeko remembered his younger brother, who had always stolen his mother's attention. "They cry and spit and wet their shorts."

Norby teased, "You and the little guy have something in common, then."

Veeko's hands contracted into meaty fists. But before he could swing, Eddie pushed him away from Norby.

The two always fought before a job — jittery nerves.

"Knock it off," Eddie said. "If anything goes wrong, it ain't gonna be because of The Plan, and it ain't gonna be because of me. It's gonna be one of you two getting a hot head. Calm down and get to work."

chapter 3

*B*aby Bink felt the stroller wheels vibrate beneath him as Gilbertine pushed him across the floor. He clutched his boo-boo in his chubby hands. Baby Bink smiled at the picture of Baby Boo's nanny pushing his stroller past the gorilla cage at the zoo.

Baby Bink wondered where he was going. He hoped he was going to the zoo. He knew something special was happening today because Mommy and Gilbertine had spent a tediously long time putting him into fancy clothes.

Baby Bink didn't like the black velvet suit or its stiff, white collar. He didn't like having his hair combed or when Mommy twisted his bangs into a big curl in the middle of his forehead. But Baby Bink didn't make a fuss. As long as he had his boo-boo he was happy.

When he looked up from his book, Bink saw Mr.

Andrews open the library's large double doors. Inside were three men who didn't look like anyone Baby Bink had ever seen before. The men did not look like the sort of grownups who would play with him. So Bink went back to looking at his boo-boo.

Suddenly the oldest man rushed across the room and put his big, ugly face right next to Bink's. His breath smelled stale and his eyelids were all puffy.

"What a gorgeous baby!" Eddie exclaimed.

Baby Bink felt shy, so he turned a page in his boo-boo. Baby Boo had left the gorilla cage and was visiting the pigs in the petting zoo. The pigs looked just like the big, ugly man.

"You must be so proud!" Eddie gushed to Gilbertine.

The nanny nodded ever so slightly. Eddie suddenly grimaced. He noticed that the young woman wore a starched, white apron. She had to be the nanny. Rich kids had nannies. Once again he'd wasted his charm on a servant!

The gangster turned his glance to Laraine and cranked up the charm several notches. "From beautiful mothers come beautiful babies."

Laraine smiled her automatic cocktail-party smile. She was only slightly flattered by Eddie's words. Laraine knew she was beautiful and did not appreciate the hired photographer making such a personal remark. He was a very odd-looking man, and she wondered vaguely if he was one of those artistic types from downtown. She knew that many strange people lived in the city, and that strange people gravitated to the arts. One had to endure their sometimes odd behavior if one wanted to purchase the fruits of their labor.

Laraine gestured with a perfectly manicured hand bearing a ring that had been in Bing's family for generations. "I'm Mrs. Cotwell."

Eddie and Norby bowed. At a loss for what to do, Veeko saluted the pretty woman. Eddie's dark eyes rolled. He knew The Plan was pure genius, but could he pull it off with two dimwits like Veeko and Norby?

"I'm Mr. Charlie," Eddie announced grandly. "This is my assistant, Mr. . . . Marcel."

Norby's nervous mouth tried to smile. *Marcel? That was a dumb, sissy name if ever he'd heard one. How dare Eddie —*

"And this is my assistant's assistant, Mr. . . . Francis," Eddie continued.

Now it was Veeko's turn to be stunned. *Francis? What kind of name was that?*

Norby grinned. Veeko's phony name was even worse than his. And Eddie had called Veeko Norby's assistant!

Before Veeko could say anything, Eddie smiled a big, oily smile and purred, "Shall we begin?"

He reached for Baby Bink, but Gilbertine instantly stepped between them. She thought these men were very strange. She had a cousin who was a downtown artist. And though he wore berets and black clothes and funny eyeglasses, he was nothing like these men. Her cousin's eyes were gentle and dreamy. These men had hard, shifty eyes. But it was not Gilbertine's place to criticize.

"I have to develop a relationship with the child, madam. He must be comfortable with me if I am to capture his delightfully youthful spirit on film," Eddie explained hastily.

Gilbertine looked from the photographer to Laraine, and for a moment resigned herself to the helplessness of being a nanny. Gilbertine loved Baby Bink with all her heart. But Laraine was the one who had the authority to make decisions. And Laraine had decided to use Downtown Baby Photographers — which meant the oily man reaching for dear little Bink.

Gilbertine smiled to herself when she saw one of Bink's hard-toed white shoes swing into the front of the photographer's pants. The man's eyes bulged with pain. Baby Bink smiled.

Clutching Bink awkwardly in his arms, the photographer waddled painfully toward the fireplace. He placed Bink in a high-backed chair around which his assistants had arranged several bright lights.

Eddie struggled to regain upright posture and to keep tears of pain out of his eyes. Eddie reminded himself that all of this — even the surprisingly hard baby shoes! — was worthwhile. *Just stick to The Plan,* Eddie told himself. *And you'll be a rich man!*

"Mr. Francis, if you could go to the vehicle and retrieve my . . . light meter?" Eddie told Veeko. Eddie wasn't sure what a light meter was, but he was pretty sure it was something photographers used. He needed some excuse to get Veeko and Norby moving.

Eddie noticed with irritation that the dignified butler was following Veeko to the door. Nosy butlers were not part of The Plan!

"Sir, if you wouldn't mind letting the fellows come and go as they please," Eddie began. "Rather than clutter this fine home with our equipment, we prefer to shuttle it in and out as needed. For the number of times the fellows have to return to the truck, you'll be wearing out your shoes accompanying them."

Eddie felt the armpits of his starched white shirt grow damp with perspiration. The old man wasn't buying it!

The butler looked at Laraine. His gaze was full of suspicion and disapproval.

Laraine sighed. She was far too busy to worry about Andrews and his stuffy, proper Cotwell ways today. "It's fine, Mr. Andrews," Laraine said. And without waiting for the butler's reply, she turned to the photographer. "I want individual photos of Baby Bink."

Eddie's eyes widened in mock delight. "Baby Bink? What an absolutely delightful name!"

"It's a pet name for Bennington," Laraine explained. She pushed away the irritation she felt at the man's overly personal style. After all, she was the one who had decided not to stick with old tried-and-true Willy. Maybe this was the way modern baby photographers behaved. At least Laraine was determined not to be as stuffy as

31

Andrews. But she did feel the need to make her desires perfectly clear. "I'd like individual photos of Baby Bink, and then I'd like a portrait of the two of us."

Eddie nodded. "Whatever you wish, however you wish," he declared.

"You've photographed the children of a number of my dear friends," Laraine said, hoping to establish a common bond.

Eddie nodded vaguely.

"Those photos are forever appearing in newspapers and magazines," Laraine chattered on.

"Yes, ma'am," Eddie agreed.

"Looking at my child, wouldn't you say he's as beautiful as a baby could be?" Laraine couldn't help bragging about Bink. He was such an adorable little bundle. Sometimes Laraine had trouble believing he was really hers.

The photographer studied Baby Bink's perfect face. Spittle dribbled between Bink's cupid lips. "Without question, as beautiful as a baby can be!" the man exclaimed.

"His picture's never been published," Laraine said with a hint of outrage.

"That can't be true!" Eddie cried. He hoped he wasn't laying it on too thick. But he knew the best way to con people was to agree with them completely.

"It's true," said Laraine.

Eddie patted Baby Bink's soft hair. "I'm sure that in the not-so-distant future, this little fella's going to be very well-known," he assured Laraine. It was all he could do not to laugh out loud. *This woman's just begging to be ripped off. She's as gullible as a kid herself.*

Bink fidgeted under Eddie's touch. Eddie removed his hand, and Gilbertine rushed forward to soothe the baby and readjust his curl.

"I want you to do your very best," Laraine instructed the photographer. "I want art. I want you to set a new standard for beauty in baby photography."

Eddie smiled. She had just handed him the excuse he needed! "I so welcome the challenge, madam. And to that end, may I ask a small favor?" Eddie paused. This part was crucial to The Plan. "May I have some time alone with the child? I need his complete attention. The great bond between you and your son, his love for you, will distract him. I need to study his marvelous little features so that I can learn how best to photograph him. He does well with persons he isn't intimate with?"

The photographer's sudden speech confused Laraine. She had not anticipated his request.

Did Bink do well with strangers? Laraine realized she did not know. She looked to Gilbertine. "Does he?"

Gilbertine addressed her reply to the photographer. She hoped the man would take the hint and let her stay in the room with Bink. "He's a friendly boy. But he may —"

"Excellent!" Eddie did not let the nanny finish.

Instead, he turned to Laraine. He had to get the mother out of the way, and Eddie knew just how.

"Madam, if I might make a suggestion, and please correct me if I'm out of order. Your garment *d'jour,* while extremely magnificent, is so colorful that I'm afraid it will dominate the photograph and detract from your natural beauty."

"I knew this outfit was too much," Laraine told Gilbertine. Then she quickly added to the photographer, "I can be changed in fifteen minutes."

Norby grinned. The boss really was a genius, like he always said. Eddie bowed. "Take all the time you need."

Gilbertine was reluctant to leave Bink alone. She hesitated in the doorway, then handed the photographer Bink's favorite picture book. "If he gets cranky, read him his book."

"Boo-boo!" Baby Bink exclaimed in delight. Maybe the funny men *were* going to read him his story!

Eddie clutched the book, trying to hide his eagerness for the nanny to leave. "How invaluable. Thank you."

Mr. Andrews pulled the double doors shut behind him. Baby Bink felt sad. Where was Mommy? Where was Gilbertine? Where was Mr. Andrews? He waited for them to pop back into the room. Peek-a-boo! But they didn't. Baby Bink's lower lip pushed out in a pout. Tears welled in his eyes. His lips parted in preparation for a great, big scream . . .

Eddie clamped his hand over Baby Bink's mouth. *Phew! Caught that just in time,* Eddie congratulated himself. *If the kid had —*

Eddie's thoughts were interrupted by a sudden and

violent eruption beneath his fingers. Something hot and gooey gushed from the rich baby's mouth.

Eddie tried to stay cool, even as his nostrils filled with the sour smell of baby spit-up.

Laraine knew just what she should wear. Unfortunately, the outfit had been packed away with the rest of her winter wardrobe. But the subdued tones of that particular wool jersey dress were just right to set off her hair and Bink's eyes. Nothing else would do! Laraine decided the photographer must be a genius after all, despite his informal manners. He had certainly been right about her outfit — too distracting for a photo session. Whatever had she been thinking of this morning? Well, at least it wasn't too late now to correct her mistake.

"Mr. Andrews!" Laraine called. "Hurry to the attic and get the winter wardrobe!"

The butler's already straight back stiffened. "Madam, that would leave the photographer unattended."

Laraine's foot stamped the marble floor. "Don't be such a stickler. What's he going to do? Steal the furniture?"

At that very moment, Norby stood in the thick shrubs outside the library window. "Gimme the kid," he said.

Eddie handed Baby Bink out the window. Then he passed Bink's storybook out to Norby as well. While Norby hurried to the van with his precious cargo, Eddie left a note on the library desk. Then he, too, rushed out to the Downtown Baby Photographers' van.

In the driver's seat, Veeko started the already warm engine. As soon as Eddie pulled the door shut behind him, they were on their way! Eddie peeled off his sticky gloves and tossed them out the window.

The van sped down the curved driveway. Baby Bink bounced happily on Norby's lap. He was in a truck! He was going to have a big adventure — just like Baby Boo!

The van rumbled off the driveway and onto one of the service roads on Eddie's diagram. Further down the quiet, wooded lane, the thugs had parked their own rusted, dented van. When they reached it, the criminals scrambled out of the Downtown Baby Photographers' vehicle. They immediately started pulling off their uniforms.

Norby winced as he yanked off his beard. Veeko forgot about his eyeglasses and got them stuck on his sweater.

"We gotta make this fast!" Eddie urged. "Gimme the keys."

Veeko reached in his pocket for the keys to the van. His hand came out full of assorted junk, change, and several keys. Veeko sorted through it as fast as he could.

Baby Bink saw the shiny keys. He loved keys! He liked to shake them and chew them. Bink reached his chubby fists toward the keys and plucked them from Veeko's palm.

Baby Bink jiggled the keys and gurgled with delight. The funny man made a funny face and grabbed for the keys, but Baby Bink's tiny hand tightened its grip.

"Knock it off, worm. Gimme the keys!" Veeko cried.

Baby Bink liked this game. He threw the keys as hard as he could. The keys went flying through the air into the forest. They landed softly on a carpet of leaves.

Veeko scowled. "What did you do that for?"

Baby Bink giggled.

Eddie felt his armpits dampen again. Losing the keys was not part of The Plan. Every second counted if they were going to make a clean getaway. "Don't just stand there, moron. Go get the keys!" Eddie shrieked.

"Hold this," Veeko said, holding the gurgling baby out to Eddie.

"I'm the boss. I don't do that," Eddie protested. He could still smell the kid's spit-up.

Veeko handed Baby Bink to Norby, then rushed into the woods. Norby regarded the child wriggling in his arms. He had never spent any time with a baby. Norby marveled at the tiny hands — each finger a perfect miniature version of Norby's own fingers. And the little guy had a great smile, even if he hardly did have any teeth. "He's kind of neat-looking, Eddie. Little junior human."

"Careful, he pukes," Eddie warned.

Norby felt Baby Bink's bottom and remarked, "He's a little humid in the shorts too."

While Eddie realized The Plan would have to be

revised to include diapers, Veeko crawled on hands and knees. He groped through the leafy underbrush. Finally, he found the keys to the van.

But before he stood up, something suddenly occurred to Veeko: a dim memory of the Boy Scout meetings Mom had forced him to attend in grade school. He stared at the dark green foliage.

"Hey, Eddie?" Veeko bellowed. "How many leaves does poison ivy got?"

"Three," Eddie replied.

Veeko was impressed. Eddie knew everything. Veeko's lips moved as he counted the waxy leaves: one, two, three. There were three leaves on each stem of the plant he'd been crawling through.

As if waiting for this knowledge to enter his brain, Veeko's hands immediately started itching. Red welts sprang up on the skin like crocuses in May. Scratching violently, Veeko emerged from the woods clutching the keys in one swollen hand.

Bink saw the funny man scratching. He laughed and laughed. Baby Bink was having an adventure — just like Baby Boo!

chapter 4

*A*s the rattling van raced into the big city, Laraine smoothed the skirt of her wool dress and hurried into the library. "I'm sorry I took so long . . ." she began. But something was wrong. Her eyes wandered from gauzy drapes to brocade chairs to leather sofa. Everything was in its proper place — but where were the photographers?

Laraine was confused. She looked to Gilbertine, who had entered the library behind her.

"They left?" Laraine asked.

Gilbertine did not answer. Her heart was in her mouth. She stared in horror at the open window. Then she spotted the note on the library desk. Gilbertine's world shrank to the size of the crudely cut-out words pasted on that white page:

WE HAVE YOUR BABY.
DON'T CALL THE POLICE.

The look of alarm on the nanny's face made Laraine nervous. A terrible truth slowly began to dawn.

"Where's Bink?" she asked.

Gilbertine's eyes filled with tears. "He's been . . . kidnapped!"

Laraine gasped. All at once her tidy world shattered, as abruptly as a crystal goblet dropped on a marble floor. Baby Bink was gone!

At that moment, Baby Bink was in the old van bouncing along a run-down city street. He saw a giant billboard with a painted coffee cup and a real clock. Bink gurgled with delight when the hands of the clock moved. Baby Bink liked tick-tocks!

Veeko's itchy, red hands turned the wheel to park the van. The clock billboard rested on the roof of the five-story building where the kidnappers lived.

Norby carried Bink up five flights of sagging stairs. "This little guy sure gets heavy!" he complained.

Eddie gritted his teeth and reminded himself, *The Plan is worth it. It has to be worth it! Please let it be worth it.*

Eddie opened several locks, then opened the door. He dropped a bag containing milk, a baby bottle, disposable diapers, baby clothes, a teddy bear, and poison-ivy cream. For the first time in a long while, Eddie

40

allowed himself to really look at the apartment he shared with Norby and Veeko. It reminded him of a line from an old Bette Davis movie his partners would be too young to remember. *What a dump!*

Newspapers, empty cans, and assorted rubbish filled the space between tattered, secondhand furniture in the drab living room. A half-wall covered in peeling paint separated that room from the cramped kitchen where Veeko heated milk in a dented saucepan. Norby deposited Bink on the scratched linoleum kitchen table and opened a plastic sack of diapers.

Eddie sank into the lumpy armchair in the living room and started reading the paper. As soon as he had flipped to the sports page, Norby called his name. Eddie rolled his eyes in disgust. Once this job was over, he'd get himself some smart partners — or better still, he'd have no partners at all. *Just me and a cold drink on some tropical beach. That's the life.*

"Hey, Eddie?" Norby repeated. "How do you tell front from back on these diapers?"

Eddie had no idea. But he was not about to admit that in front of the boys. "Are there pockets on the front?"

"Very funny," Norby snapped.

Eddie hadn't been trying to be funny.

"The front and back's the same," Norby whined.

"Then it probably don't make a difference," Eddie replied. "Put him in them regular baby clothes. That

41

fancy velvet suit's a dead giveaway that he's a rich kid." *And no rich kid belonged in this dump, that was for sure!*

While Norby struggled to put on a fresh diaper, Bink looked out the kitchen window. Pigeons strutted on the crumbling ledge. Bink pointed at the pigeons excitedly. There were birds, just like in his boo-boo! Baby Bink loved the birds in his boo-boo.

Norby ignored Bink's pointing fingers. He was bent over trying to get the wiggly baby into the secondhand striped pullover shirt and faded blue baby overalls. Norby had no idea babies moved so much, or that their little legs could kick so hard. He wondered why the overalls had to have so many darn little snaps.

Veeko's tongue stuck out of his mouth with the effort of pouring the milk from the saucepan into the baby bottle. He felt like one of those scientists in the movies on TV. The bottle felt very warm against his swollen palm. He yelled to Eddie, "How do I know this milk won't burn the kid's throat?"

"Try it on some skin first," Eddie advised over his newspaper. Would these two ever let him read the boxing results?

Veeko nodded. The boss really did know everything. He shook the bottle over Norby's neck.

"AIYEEE!" Norby shrieked. He snapped upright and rubbed his burned neck. "What's the matter with you?" he yelled at Veeko.

"I better let it cool off," Veeko concluded.

Norby slapped the side of Veeko's head. Bink saw the slap and laughed.

Norby was pleased to see the baby's sunny smile. "You like that?"

Bink clapped his tiny hands together and giggled.

Norby called across the room. "Eddie! Watch the baby."

Jeez! They didn't let him alone for a second. Eddie lowered his newspaper and watched as Norby slapped Veeko again.

"Hey!" Veeko protested.

Baby Bink giggled again.

Eddie was glad to see the boys had found a way to amuse the brat. "Very good," he told Norby. "Now see if it works the other way."

Veeko slapped Norby. Bink laughed in delight. This was a fun adventure indeed! Baby Bink liked these funny men.

Eddie turned another page of his newspaper and settled as comfortably as he could in the lumpy chair. Soon he would have a real chair with an automatic footstool, just like they advertised on TV. But first, they had to pull off The Plan.

Eddie called to Norby, "Put him in the bedroom. The more he sleeps, the less attention he draws from the neighbors. And keep an eye on him. That little spit-up machine is my retirement money."

Baby Bink sucked his bottle as the funny man carried him into the dingy bedroom. Norby put the baby down on the bed against the window.

"Nappy-nap time," Norby said. He pulled the teddy bear out from under his arm and tucked it in beside Bink. "Go to sleep real nice. Mr. Teddy Bear's been up all night drinking with the Barbie dolls. He needs his rest."

Baby Bink threw his bottle aside. Norby put the bottle back in the baby's mouth. Bink spit it out again. This was fun!

"You gotta drink your milk if you're gonna grow up to be big and strong," Norby said.

Baby Bink spit out the bottle. He didn't like it as much as his bottle at home. It tasted funny.

"Nice manners on you, kid," Norby said. Then he put the bottle back in the baby's mouth again. "Drink your bottle; take your nap."

Bink tossed the bottle once more on the floor.

Norby gritted his teeth in frustration. No wonder people said being a parent was the toughest job in the world. This stank — not to mention the diaper!

"Eddie?" Norby called into the living room. "Any suggestions on how you get these things to eat and sleep?"

Eddie lowered his paper again. "Sing him a song."

Norby sat on the bed and cleared his throat. He tried to remember the songs his mother sang to him, but that was a long time ago. He suddenly recalled one of those stupid poems the teachers used to make kids memorize at school. Norby sang:

"Mary had a little lamb,
Little lamb, little lamb.
Mary had a little lamb,
Its hair was white as snow.
And every which way that Mary went,
The lamb was right behind her.
It followed her to work one day,
work one day, work one day.
Followed her to work one day.
And Mary lost her job.

Norby stopped singing to call to Eddie. "What else did Mary's little lamb do?"

Eddie closed his paper in disgust and tried to think.

Veeko tried too. "It went to work with her," he offered.

"I did that already," Norby said.

"Didn't he put Humpty Dumpty back together again?" Eddie suggested.

Veeko shook his head. He couldn't believe he knew something the boss didn't know. But he figured it had been a long time since Eddie was a kid.

"That was Nat King Cole," Veeko corrected.

Eddie knew whatever Veeko said had to be wrong. "Nat King Cole stuck his finger in the pie and yanked out a bird."

Veeko was still wondering about the big, broken egg. "How can a lamb put a Humpty together? They ain't got fingers!"

Eddie had the solution. "Norby? Knock off the singing and read him his storybook." Eddie realized he had never seen Norby reading — not even a racing form. So he teased, "If you can."

Norby stretched out on the bed beside Baby Bink and opened the well-thumbed picture book. He flipped the book open at random.

It had been years since Norby had read anything. And now that he saw the printed words on the page, Norby remembered why. Reading was hard! It took a while to recognize the black squiggles as letters and to sound out the words those letters formed. Norby read, "Nan . . . ny and Baby Boo strol . . . led th . . . rough the great, big de . . . part . . . ment store. How many, many things there were to buy!"

Norby looked up from the picture of the big department store and into Baby Bink's round blue eyes. "If I was writing this book, it would say, 'How many, many things there were to steal.'"

Bink clapped his tiny hands. He loved his boo-boo, even if the funny man didn't read as well as Nanny Gilbertine.

Norby bent over the page once more and read. "Nan . . . ny was very watchful of Baby Boo. It would be so, so easy for Baby Boo to get lost in the big de . . . part . . . ment store."

Norby chuckled and added slyly, "Or kidnapped."

chapter 5

· · · · · · · · · · · · · · · ·

*K*idnapped! Laraine still could not believe her precious Baby Bink had been kidnapped. She pinched herself in order to stop pretending that this was all just a dreadful nightmare, even as she watched the police cars park in the gravel driveway.

It's real, she told herself. As real as the grim, middle-aged man marching through the door behind Mr. Andrews. *Oh Andrews! If only I had listened to you!* Laraine thought for the millionth time that day.

Laraine pulled herself up out of an ocean of regret long enough to greet the man who flashed an ID badge in a cheap leather wallet. Laraine stared blankly at the badge. *How could it be that police officers were in her home?*

"Special Agent Dale Grissom, Federal Bureau of Investigation," the man said in a low voice. He looked tired and impatient at the same time. His summer suit was neatly pressed, but it was obviously not an expensive one.

Laraine took a deep breath and patiently answered the agent's questions. Her lips moved and words dribbled out. But all the while Laraine wondered how she could possibly go on living if Bink wasn't returned home soon.

Laraine watched with dull, shell-shocked eyes as various police specialists dusted the library for fingerprints and combed the plush furniture and Oriental carpet for stray hairs.

Later, she was dimly aware of having changed out of her wool dress and into trousers and a simple blouse. She realized Dr. Phillips was in the master bedroom with her and Gilbertine. Laraine didn't remember calling the family physician and realized Andrews or Gilbertine must have done that.

Laraine didn't want a doctor. She did not want to feel better. All she wanted — more than anything she'd ever wanted in her whole life — was for Baby Bink to come home.

Laraine had never known this feeling before. The pain in her heart was as sharp as steel. She no longer cared about herself. She didn't give a hoot what she looked like. If someone told her that all the clothes in her closet had just turned to dust, she couldn't have cared less. If they told her she'd never have a credit card or go shopping again, Laraine wouldn't have blinked an eye. Her mind was empty except for one thing: BABY BINK!

"Laraine?" Dr. Phillips was concerned. He was accustomed to treating tennis elbow, high blood pressure, even heart attacks. He had little experience with shock. Phillips filled a syringe with a sedative and squirted out enough liquid to clear the needle of air. The physician noted with growing concern that his patient completely ignored him.

"Did you tell Mr. Andrews to bring my car out?" Laraine asked Gilbertine.

"Yes. But where can you go?" the nanny wondered. In the absence of Baby Bink, the nurturing young woman naturally turned her attention to her employer, who certainly seemed to be in great need of care. "You don't know —"

Laraine interrupted. "My baby's been stolen! I'm not going to sit here and have Dr. Phillips sedate me, and you two pamper me and lie to me. I'm going to look for my baby!"

Without another word, Laraine stomped out of the room. But before she could cross the marble entrance hall, Agent Grissom stopped her. "Mrs. Cotwell? I'd like to ask you a few questions."

"Talk to the nanny. I'm leaving," Laraine replied brusquely.

"I'd rather you didn't go," the agent said firmly. "I need you here."

Laraine sighed impatiently. He couldn't need her. She

was useless. Hadn't she proved that already? It was all her fault! Guilt washed over Laraine again. Guilt and shame for the vanity that had prompted her to want Bink's picture in the paper. The young woman who had sipped her English breakfast tea that morning was no longer, and her frivolous dreams had disappeared with her.

"Don't coddle me, Mr. Grissom," Laraine said.

"There are five million people in the city, thousands of places your boy could be." The agent tried to sound more patient than he felt. The last thing he needed was this rich woman taking the law into her own hands. Who knew what kind of trouble she could wind up in while driving through bad neighborhoods, already hysterical with fear. "It would be pointless and dangerous for you to try and search for your baby," Grissom added more gently.

Laraine had no thoughts of her own safety. "I can't just sit here and feel sorry for myself."

"We're going to need information from you," Agent Grissom began. "I'd like to keep you close by. I've been through a number of these cases. I understand how you feel."

Laraine's eyes were wild. "Have you ever lost a child?"

Grissom's gaze dropped to the floor. "No, ma'am," he admitted quietly.

"Then you can't possibly know how I feel," Laraine replied.

Grissom felt bad. He was more sympathetic than many of his fellow agents. Still, he sometimes forgot that what to him was just another case was to this woman a personal tragedy. "I apologize," he said, sounding for the first time more like a man than an agent. "Will you stay here, please? For your baby's sake?"

Laraine hesitated. She knew Grissom was right. What was the point of driving all over creation without a clue as to where Bink might be hidden? Perhaps the urge to DO SOMETHING, ANYTHING was just another selfish impulse. Laraine nodded slowly.

Agent Grissom looked into Laraine's tortured eyes. Then he quickly went back to business. "I need the baby's hospital records and a recent photograph."

Laraine did not believe her heart could hurt any more. But the irony of the agent's request brought a fresh stab of pain. *Oh, Bink — where are you?*

At that moment, Baby Bink was in the shabby bedroom of the crooks' apartment. Norby had fallen fast asleep under the soothing spell of *Baby's Day Out.*

Bink watched the pigeons strut and peck on the rusty fire escape. He stuck his head through the open window for a better view. *Coo, coo* went the big gray birds.

Baby Bink looked up, down, and all around. He saw the alley five stories beneath him through the wrought-iron slats. He watched the pigeons fly up to the roof.

Bink couldn't fly, but he could climb. One chubby limb in front of the other, Bink slowly crawled up the

51

fire escape to the roof. He heard police sirens shrieking.

Baby Bink didn't know the sirens belonged to three police cars leading his daddy's limousine home. Bink wasn't thinking about Daddy at all. He had no idea Bing was suffering the worst anguish of his life. Bink only knew that he liked to watch the birds that looked just like the birds in his boo-boo.

Following the flock, Bink crawled across the grimy roof. He stopped at a dirt-smeared skylight at the foot of a brick chimney. TIME FOR FLAVOR announced the sign with the big clock. Bink pulled himself onto the raised skylight and peeked down through a broken pane of glass.

Bink saw the funny men who had brought him on his big adventure. Eddie sat in his lumpy chair trying to complete the crossword puzzle in his newspaper. Veeko sat next to Eddie, biting his nails. Bink watched the big thug chew a nail, then spit, chew a nail, then spit.

Eddie could not swallow his irritation any longer. "Do you gotta do that?"

Veeko replied, "I like to look nice."

Eddie felt his blood pressure rise. "You gotta spit?"

Veeko didn't understand why the boss was always so grumpy. He wondered if grumpiness was part of being smart. "I don't know about you, but I don't eat pieces of my body," Veeko explained.

Baby Bink grinned down at the two funny men. Bink liked to watch them almost as much as he liked watching the birds. He grinned. A thin strand of drool fell through the broken skylight down to the apartment below.

The drool landed on Eddie's neck just as Veeko spit out another shred of fingernail. Eddie glared at Veeko. The younger thug stopped chewing and looked up. "What?"

Eddie slapped Veeko's head.

Veeko was stunned. "What'd I do?"

"You spit on me!" Eddie shrieked.

"I did not!" Veeko denied.

"Someone did, and you're the only one in the room," Eddie said, rubbing his neck again with disgust.

Baby Bink was delighted. His new friends got funnier all the time. This really was a great adventure! Bink pounded his tiny fist on the glass and giggled with delight.

Eddie and Veeko heard the noise and tilted their heads up. Eddie stared into Bink's delighted blue eyes.

No, Eddie thought desperately. *It can't be!* Eddie shot a glance into the bedroom, then stared at Veeko who stared right back at him. Then they both looked up once more.

Eddie's eyes bulged in amazement. It couldn't be — but it was! The kid was on the roof!

Just as Eddie came to that terrible realization, Bink dropped out of sight. Eddie's stomach clenched at the thought of his retirement money rolling off the roof. He was on his feet so fast it made his head spin.

With Veeko at his heels, Eddie scrambled to the bedroom. He flung open the door and found Norby sound asleep with the teddy bear clutched in his arms.

Eddie screamed at the top of his lungs. "YOU JERK!"

Norby popped up and hissed, "Shh! You'll wake the baby!"

"THE BABY'S ON THE ROOF!" Eddie roared.

Norby was confused. How could the baby be on the roof? Norby had just been reading to the little tyke when . . . Norby looked from the bed to the open window. He shrank from Eddie's glare. *Oops!* Norby thought. *Why do things always have to go wrong?*

The men hurried up to the roof where Bink was having a wonderful time. He had crawled to the side of the building that overlooked the big city. It looked just like the picture in his boo-boo — only it was real!

Bink gurgled with excitement. He pulled himself closer to the edge of the roof to get a better view. He pointed his chubby fingers. A few blocks from the apartment was a construction site. Bink saw big trucks carrying sand and steel. He saw a churning cement mixer. It was just like the construction site Baby Boo visited in his boo-boo — only it was real!

Baby Bink wanted to visit a construction site too. He crawled along the edge of the roof until he came to a roofer's board. The board went from the roof of the crooks' building to the next building, which was closer to the construction site. Bink crawled fearlessly across the board. His chubby fingers clutched the sides of the thin plank rocking under his shifting weight.

Bink almost reached the neighboring roof as Eddie, Veeko, and Norby ran to the edge of theirs. Eddie leaned out to see the baby. Tipped up by Bink's weight, the end of the board slapped Eddie under the chin. He fell down — hard!

Norby and Veeko helped him get back on his feet.

"You okay?" Veeko asked.

Eddie felt a bit bruised and dizzy. He shook his head to try to clear the pain and get those pesky stars out of his eyes. "I'm all right," he growled.

But just then, Bink reached the next roof. When he crawled off the board, it went flying up, then down — right on Eddie's head! Another galaxy exploded behind Eddie's eyes as the plank spun down five stories to land in the street with a loud KA-THUNK.

Eddie could not remember the last time his head hurt this much — not even on the morning after a late poker night. But he was determined to get that baby back, and so were Norby and Veeko.

Norby judged the distance to the next roof. It wasn't that far. He turned to Eddie. "We're gonna jump, okay?"

Eddie felt groggy, but he nodded. How else could they get the kid back?

Veeko crouched and dug his feet into the roof, ready to spring. "One . . ."

Norby braced himself. "Two . . ."

Together they cried "Three!" as they leaped across the void. Norby and Veeko landed together on the other roof.

Eddie jumped too, but he didn't make it. His legs scrambled. His arms flailed. And he fell, like the helpless dreamer in a nightmare.

Eddie dropped between the two buildings, then landed with a THUD on an old woman's window air conditioner. The woman looked out of her kitchen window and dropped her spoon.

For a moment, Eddie sat on top of the air conditioner. He felt his heart start beating again. Then he felt himself falling once more as the machine slipped out of the window.

Eddie landed on a window-box garden one floor below the old lady's apartment. But just as he was trying to figure out how to get inside that window, Eddie felt the garden giving way beneath him. *Not again!* he thought, just before he dropped into space.

One floor below the garden, Eddie saw a bird feeder stuck to the window with four suction cups. *Maybe I can grab it!* he thought hopefully.

Eddie's frantic, fumbling hands reached the bird feeder. He watched in horror as the first suction cup went POP, then the second, third, and fourth. POP, POP, POP!

Veeko and Norby winced as they watched their leader's fall continue. Eddie dropped through lines of hanging laundry, past TV and radio antennae, and smashed into more air conditioners.

Eddie finally landed with a giant crash on a bunch of metal garbage cans. All the things he had knocked loose in his downfall showered on Eddie in a hail of bricks, plants, clothes, and broken air conditioners.

He hadn't felt this bad since his last knockout in professional boxing, when he took that left to the temple that sent the mat rushing up to meet him.

"Ed!" Veeko shrieked when he saw his boss. The younger thugs had raced downstairs and around to the alley where their leader lay sprawled on top of the garbage cans. Eddie was covered in potting soil from head to toes. His ripped shirt hung out of the tattered trousers pushed up past his skinned knees.

Norby and Veeko helped Eddie to his feet. They led their dazed leader to a bench at a bus stop.

"Ed? You all right?" Veeko asked.

Norby shook his head. Sometimes Veeko really was too much to believe. "How can he be all right? He fell off a building. He's probably got contusions, concussions, infractions, infusions . . ."

Eddie was indeed miserable. Stars had given way to comets and asteroids all whizzing past his eyes at light speed. No, Eddie was not feeling well at all.

But Bink was having the time of his life. From the roof, Bink had crawled into an open kitchen window. He loved exploring new places. Bink crawled across the slick linoleum floor until he reached the carpeted living room. Bink crawled across that room too.

He had just reached the front door when it was pushed open. Bink fell down on his bottom. While the door was still open, Bink crawled out. This was fun!

Baby Bink crawled down the hall to the elevator. Inside was a delivery man who carried a big box. Bink crawled into the elevator just as the doors closed. Because of the package he was carrying, the delivery man didn't see the baby. Bink enjoyed the ride down to the first floor. *Whee!*

Bink crawled outside the apartment building. Then he saw a big bus, just like the one in his favorite book.

"Boo-boo!" Baby Bink cried, pointing at the bus.

Whoosh! The bus doors opened. Bink crawled among the passengers waiting to board the bus.

On the bench behind the bus, the comets and asteroids faded from Eddie's mind as he listened to Norby and Veeko chatter.

"When we seen you fall, our thoughts were with you and your family should you not survive," Norby said gravely.

"I prayed," Veeko added solemnly.

"Shut up," Eddie said impatiently. "Where's the kid?"

Norby looked at Veeko. Veeko looked at Norby. They had been so busy worrying about Eddie, they'd forgotten all about Baby Bink!

The young thugs both caught sight of the departing bus at the same time. Bink sat on the high, black steps inside the bus. He waved bye-bye to Eddie, Norby, and Veeko through the clear panels in the rumbling vehicle's door.

Eddie squinted, not believing what he was seeing. *No, it can't be,* he reasoned. How could a baby get down from a roof and onto a bus all by himself? Not only was the impossible happening, it was pouring like a personal rain cloud down on Eddie's throbbing head.

Eddie watched the bus rumble off. Exhaust shrouded the advertisement on its back for CHANNEL 3 NEWS AT NOON. The only news Eddie wanted to hear right then was that he, Norby, and Veeko had gotten the kid back.

Though every inch of skin and every muscle ached, Eddie ran to the van and hurled himself into the driver's seat. As the van raced off, Norby slammed the passenger's door and braced himself against the dashboard. Veeko bounced around the back like a small rubber ball at the end of an elastic string.

Eddie swerved madly through the late morning traffic. Horns blared as he switched into the wrong lane, driving against the traffic to CATCH THAT BUS!

chapter 6

*C*arl, the bus driver, whistled a happy tune. So far, his shift was going well. Passengers had deposited exact change in the slot. No one had been mugged, or gotten sick, or needed directions translated into Latvian. No water mains had exploded. The weather was bright and clear. Traffic was congested, noisy, irritating — all in all, not a bad summer day in the city.

But what was that? Carl looked again in his rear-view mirror. Some maniac's van was heading down the wrong side of the street straight for his bus!

Why my shift? Carl thought, feeling his ulcer kick in. *Maybe if I ignore it, the van will go away.*

So the driver continued on his route as usual. He didn't see the baby sitting on the bus steps because his view was blocked by a large woman. Her body filled the aisle, squeezing between the metal poles that separated the driver's area from the seats. She arranged her many bundles in the stairwell, preparing to get off at the next stop. The woman clutched a wooden purse studded with seashells and rested her big tote on the step beside Baby Bink.

Whee! Bink rocked from side to side when the bus turned. He tumbled into the tote full of clean laundry. Bink loved the smell of fresh clothes. They reminded him of Nanny Gilbertine. This ride was even more fun than the elevator!

Carl glanced around as he eased onto the brakes. He was glad to see the crazy van driver was gone.

Or was he? At that moment, Eddie turned down an alley. The old van shook and rattled as if it would break apart at any moment.

"Slow down!" Norby screamed.

Veeko's voice trembled as he bounced hard on his bottom. "Watch the potholes!"

But nothing and nobody was going to stop Eddie from getting that kid! He sped down the alley with the wheel vibrating wildly under his hands. Eddie saw the bus and slammed on the brakes. The van skidded out of the alley and onto the sidewalk right in front of the bus stop.

Carl felt the shock absorbers ease as the big woman waddled off the bus carrying her bundles. Eddie flung himself out of the van. He ran to the bus, but was slowed by his bumps and bruises. Norby and Veeko scrambled past him.

Norby reached the bus just as it started to pull away. "STOOOOOOOPPPP!" he shouted.

Carl was surprised by the desperate young man's cry. *Jeez! Didn't the guy know another bus would come this way in seven minutes? What was the rush? Some people just couldn't wait for anything.*

The driver hit the brakes and opened the door. The breathless young man stuck his head inside and blurted, "Did a baby get off this bus? A little guy about two feet tall? It's an emergency."

Carl thought for a moment. *A baby. Had one of his passengers been carrying a baby today?* He remembered a red-headed toddler who'd screamed his head off all the way from Third Street — no, that was yesterday.

"I didn't have anybody today with a baby," said the driver.

Norby shook his head. "He was by himself."

Carl's face turned red with anger. *Another nut! The city was full of them. What kind of person would delay his route with some nonsense about a baby riding a bus by himself?*

The driver yanked the lever, and the bus door shut in Norby's face. Before he pulled back into traffic, Carl picked up his radio. Maybe the young man was a harmless nut, but maybe something bad was going on. Just to be on the safe side, the driver decided to report the incident.

After a crackle of static, the driver said, "This is Carl in 157. You know anything about a missing baby?"

While Carl talked to his dispatcher, Norby and Veeko told Eddie the bad news. "What?" Eddie squealed.

Norby shrugged. "He must have got off."

Eddie scowled. This job had started so well and now — Eddie's thoughts were interrupted by the big woman squeezing between him and Veeko.

"If you wouldn't park your van on the sidewalk, people could get by a lot easier," the fat woman complained.

"If you'd limit yourself to a couple of pork roasts a day, you wouldn't have to worry about it," Veeko replied.

The woman glared at Veeko, ignoring what he proudly considered to be a very snappy retort.

"You heard me!" Veeko shouted. "Some people . . ."

The big woman turned her back on the rude thug. Bink popped his head out of her tote bag.

Veeko's jaw dropped in mid-sentence. He stared, unable to speak as the woman walked around the corner with Bink peeking out of her sack.

Veeko turned to his partners.

"Maybe the little squirt fell off the bus," Norby suggested lamely.

Eddie fumed, not knowing what to do next. The kid was gone. They'd stolen him fair and square and somehow . . .

"I saw him!" Veeko cried.

Eddie was shocked out of his misery. "Huh?"

"He was in the big broad's purse!" Veeko exclaimed.

The thugs ran around the corner. The woman was

easy to spot. She lumbered down the street carrying her bundles, and the criminals quickly caught up with her. They reached for the large tote slung over her shoulder.

Bink snuggled down deep among the clean clothes. When Eddie peeked inside the bag, all he could see were sheets, shirts, and towels.

The fat woman sensed someone following her. She tightened her grip on her wooden purse and looked in a store window. She saw her reflection, with Eddie, Norby, and Veeko's reflections skulking behind her.

The big woman had lived in the city all her life. She knew how to take care of herself.

Eddie's hand reached for the tote bag's straps. As he did, the woman turned, swinging her wooden purse like a gladiator's mace. The sharp seashells smashed into Eddie's head. The lock sprang open, and the woman's makeup, wallet, keys, and other items splattered on the sidewalk before the fallen thug.

Veeko lunged at the lady. She dropped her tote to free her arms for battle. She was too busy to care that her clean laundry spilled on the sidewalk — or to notice the cute baby fall out with the clothes and crawl away.

The woman grabbed Veeko by the neck and squeezed him under her arm in a wrestler's headlock. The woman was determined to let the three thugs know they had just tried to rob the wrong person. Whatever they could dish out, she could give back — and more!

Veeko gasped for air. He felt like his neck was in a

giant vise made of human flesh. His eyes fell on the spilled laundry tote. "THE BAG!" he shouted to Norby.

The other thief reached for the tote. The woman saw him and a slow grin spread across her massive face. So they were going to play it two against one, were they? She was ready for them!

The woman quickly flipped Veeko onto his back. While stars spun around Veeko's head, she grabbed Norby by the collar and the seat of his pants and heaved him into the street. The thugs scrambled to their feet and ran away.

The woman felt faintly disappointed. She'd just started having fun. "Chicken!" she called after the departing thieves. Then she bent down to retrieve her scattered belongings.

Farther down the block, Bink stopped crawling and looked up. His eyes grew round with wonder and delight. Here was a big store, just like the one in his boo-boo!

Bink crawled toward the department store's brass and glass revolving door. Dozens of busy shoppers marched past him. He watched the parade of shoes and gurgled happily. "Boo-boo!"

Bink crawled through the spinning door and found himself on the store's huge main floor. There was so much to look at! He didn't know what to explore first.

Suddenly, Bink saw a familiar sight. The wheels of a stroller rolled past him. A baby girl looked at Bink from her stroller seat. Baby Bink crawled after her. He liked making new friends.

The baby girl's stroller stopped at Mother Goose Corner, a small day care center staffed by teenage girls. While parents shopped, the young baby-sitters changed diapers, read out loud, and doled out cookies and bottles, all under cheerful paintings of cartoon characters.

Baby Bink followed the baby girl inside. He crawled toward a changing table. Bink liked the smell of talcum powder.

The teenage sitter was tired of the smell of talcum powder. But summer jobs were hard to find. She wished it was her turn to read out loud. That was definitely better than diaper duty. She sighed.

The girl finished dusting powder on the latest bottom, expertly attached the diaper tapes, and put the baby back in its stroller.

"Next!" she called wearily.

Then the sitter spotted Baby Bink. She lifted him onto the changing table. "You got a surprise for me?" she asked.

Bink grinned. The sitter groaned. She knew what that smile meant.

Soon Baby Bink was wearing a fresh diaper and his bottom smelled of talcum powder. He crawled happily away from Mother Goose Corner. Baby Bink had lots to explore!

Bink crawled toward the revolving door. On the sidewalk outside the big department store, a pretty reporter named Ronnie Lee prepared to make her broadcast for the News at Noon.

The show filled the television screens in the display window of an electronics store where Eddie, Veeko, and Norby were catching their breath after the fat woman's attack.

"You guys are worthless," Eddie wheezed. His bruises pulsed with pain. He felt like he'd just gone ten rounds with two heavyweights packing lead in their gloves.

"I'm getting sick of your insults," Veeko groaned. His back felt like elephants had been using it for a trampoline.

"Then why don't you quit?" Eddie suggested.

Veeko smelled a rat. "And let you two have all the money?"

The woman had whipped almost the last shred of hope out of Norby. "What money?" he demanded. "The kid's gone."

Norby's remark was the subject of Ronnie Lee's report. "There's no official word from police, but sources tell us that the sixteen-month-old baby boy was abducted from his Wallington Hills home at approximately ten o'clock this morning."

All over the city, people heard the news and felt concern for Baby Bink. A worn-out, gray-haired man watched the news from his front porch. Roger Baines saw the picture of adorable Baby Bink, and it gave him an idea. While he listened to the rest of Ronnie Lee's report, Roger looked up his street to a group of children playing at the curb.

"Police are reportedly looking for a baby photographer who was in the home at the time of the abduction," Ronnie Lee continued on the man's television set.

"We have confirmed that a photographer and two assistants from the Downtown Baby Photographers' studio on the North Side were scheduled to photograph the missing child at the Wallington Hills estate today. A spokesman for the photography studio declined to comment . . ." the reporter's voice droned on.

But Roger wasn't listening. He was on the telephone. Roger Baines had never had a lucky day in his life. The world was full of rich, happy people. Roger figured it was his turn to get a piece of the pie.

chapter 7

*B*aby Bink crawled out the big store's revolving door. It patted his bottom. This was fun!

Bink saw the pretty lady with the microphone. He heard her voice, but he didn't understand that she was talking about his daddy.

"Earlier I attempted to reach millionaire Bennington Cotwell at his downtown office," Ronnie Lee said, just as Baby Bink crawled between her ankles.

Then Bink saw something wonderful! It was a bright yellow taxi cab, just like in the one in the picture in his favorite book.

"Boo-boo!" Bink cried as he crawled toward the yellow car.

A woman with lots of packages was heading for the taxi too. She opened the door, but she didn't see Baby Bink.

One of Bink's little feet got stuck on the cord to Ronnie Lee's microphone. The reporter said, "A spokesman for Mr. Cotwell's firm said Cotwell was unavailable for —"

Just then the microphone went flying out of Ronnie's hand. She bent down to pick it up, and the cameraman followed her with his lens.

If she had been looking at the television set just then, Laraine Cotwell would have seen Bink crawling on the sidewalk near Ronnie Lee's microphone. But as it was, tears blurred Laraine's eyes and she turned away from the TV, too sad to watch the report about her missing son.

At least Bing was with her now. His muscular arms circled her shaking shoulders.

"We have to be strong," Bing said, though his own voice was thick with unshed tears. "We have to keep our faith."

Laraine had rarely seen her husband so serious and tender. It reminded her of the night of Baby Bink's birth — and that brought a fresh shower of sobs. The thought of little Bink out there somewhere among strangers was almost too horrible to bear. "He's so small, so helpless," Laraine said.

Bing's arms tightened around her. He wished there was something more he could do. But for now he could only hold her — and hope they would soon see their son again.

To their amazement, Eddie, Norby, and Veeko saw Baby Bink, large as life on the color TVs in the electronics store window. The thieves looked over their shoulders and saw that the Channel 3 news van was parked in front of the big department store.

The wheels in Veeko's mind rolled slowly over the problem. *If the baby was on the TV show, and the TV show was being broadcast from outside the department store . . . the baby was outside the department store!*

Veeko, Eddie, and Norby's eyes scanned the crowded street lined with taxis and other midday traffic. They noticed a middle-aged woman getting into a taxi. But they didn't see Baby Bink climbing into the cab with her — and neither did the woman because she was holding so many bags and bundles.

Eddie and his assistants ran into the street. Brakes squealed and angry horns blared at the careless jaywalkers. The thieves stopped halfway to the opposite curb. Bink waved to them from the taxi window as it pulled away from the department store.

For a moment, Eddie wondered if he was going to faint. So far today he had kidnapped a baby, lost the baby, fallen off a five-story building, been beaten up by a fat woman, found the baby, and lost the baby again. Eddie watched his hope for a rich retirement enter the rushing stream of traffic.

Eddie's near-fainting spell passed as quickly as it had come. He sprang into action! In seconds, the old van was chasing Bink's cab. Eddie gripped the steering wheel as if it was a life preserver. *Had the world gone mad? Since when did babies hail cabs?*

Eddie knew only one thing. Whatever had happened, no way was it his fault. So he scolded Norby and Veeko. "I can't believe this. The kid's only a year old, and he's already smarter than the two of you combined."

Norby and Veeko looked at each other. They hated it when Eddie picked on them, which was almost all the time. But neither one had the courage to stand up to their boss.

"You know," Eddie ranted. "It ain't the wisest strategy to kidnap a baby and then let the darn thing loose on the streets. Babies crawling in traffic tend to draw attention, don't you think?"

As the van followed Bink's taxi, two unmarked police cars and a limousine sped down a quiet street lined with run-down row houses. On the sagging front porch of one of those houses was an old television set belonging to Roger Baines.

Roger switched off the set when he saw the limo. To him it was a bakery delivery truck coming to bring him his share of the pie.

Roger waited coolly while Laraine, Bing, and Agent Grissom climbed up the rickety porch steps. He didn't even get out of his chair.

"I seen the baby," Roger said by way of greeting. He had done his share of lying in his lifetime. Convincing two desperate parents of what they wanted to hear was going to be a piece of cake.

Agent Grissom asked, "Where?"

"Outside," Roger replied with what he hoped sounded like a casual tone of voice. "On the curb across the street."

"Where'd he go?" Grissom demanded.

Roger knew he had to make his play now. "Funny thing. I don't remember."

Agent Grissom's fists clenched. Whenever a case involved big money, rats like Baines scampered out of the woodwork looking for crumbs. "Maybe we'll take a little ride," the agent said. His deep voice growled with menace. "See if you remember then."

Bing suddenly grasped the situation. "You want money?"

Grissom held up his hand to stop Mr. Cotwell. Roger watched the interplay between the agent, the millionaire, and his pretty wife.

Then Laraine spoke. "That's what he wants. Pay him."

Roger suppressed a smile as Bing reached for his wallet. These folks had dollars piled to the sky. Why shouldn't Roger Baines take a few off the top?

Agent Grissom said firmly, "Mr. Cotwell, we'll deal with this."

But Bing was determined to leave no stone unturned. If this unpleasant man had a lead, no price was too high. Money meant nothing to him now. All Bing wanted was Baby Bink.

Bing tossed two hundred-dollar bills at Roger.

"Don't worry about it," Bing told Grissom. Then he turned his attention to the scruffy witness. "Where'd the baby go?"

First, Roger collected the money. He had never seen a hundred-dollar bill before. He didn't recognize the man whose portrait was printed on the face.

Clutching the two bills, Roger said, "Across the street. In the building."

He didn't elaborate. Roger was determined to milk the situation for all it was worth.

Bing pulled another crisp hundred out of his wallet. Roger wondered bitterly if the man always carried so much cash. *I could probably live for a year on what this guy spends on golf clubs,* Roger realized, scooping up the bill.

Roger felt Agent Grissom glaring at him, and knew it was time to quit while he was ahead.

"McCray," Roger said. Then he hastily added, "No guarantee. I don't know your kid. I seen a strange face looking like they said on the news. I called 'cause I care."

Roger grinned. He knew that sentimental stuff would really sell the con. At least it would to the parents, if not the cop. Still, Roger was relieved when the three went down the porch steps, relieved, but faintly regretful. He wondered if he should have held out for more.

Roger took the three hundred-dollar bills from his pocket and regarded them fondly. He noticed that the portly face staring back at him belonged to Franklin.

Good old Ben. Roger would never forget that.

Several FBI agents charged up the six flights of creaking stairs before Agent Grissom, Laraine, and Bing. Laraine was dimly aware of the stale smell of cooked cabbage, dirty diapers, and smoke. Her designer sneakers jogged past empty bottles, junk-food wrappers, and cigarette stubs as she raced up the worn stairs.

Ilene McCray heard the sound of many footsteps pounding up the stairs outside. She hoped it wasn't trouble. But in this neighborhood, trouble was never far away.

Ilene McCray was only halfway through her thirties. Her feet felt like seventy. Hard work and lack of sleep had taken their toll on the rest of her as well. It hadn't been an easy life so far, but Ilene found joy where she could, mostly in the smiles of her children.

A newborn baby stirred on Ilene's hip. Her little ones were finally down for their nap. The older children watched cartoons in the living room. This was usually one of the rare, peaceful moments in Ilene's day. The footsteps stopped. Someone pounded on her door. So much for peace.

Ilene peeked out. An FBI identification badge flashed before her eyes. A man's deep voice demanded gruffly, "Your name's McCray?"

Ilene's stomach flip-flopped nervously. What could the FBI want with her? She'd never done anything wrong.

"We're looking for a missing child," the agent said.

Ilene felt confused. Who would steal a child? Goodness knows she had plenty of her own.

"These are my kids," she stated defensively.

"You mind if we look around?" the agent persisted.

Ilene didn't like opening her door to strangers, even ones that flashed FBI badges. But she was afraid to say no. Couldn't they throw you in jail for that or something? Who would take care of the kids if she was in jail?

Ilene stepped back to let the agents enter. She stared at Bing and Laraine, who followed behind. Their clothes looked like something out of a magazine. Cops couldn't dress like that. Ilene wondered who the rich people were.

The agents' trained eyes quickly scanned the faces of the children huddled on the shabby couch, then they fanned out to search the only other rooms — the small, dingy kitchen and a single bedroom.

Agent Grissom was pretty sure they were on a wild-goose chase, but at this stage in the case they had to follow all leads. He addressed the puzzled woman. "Hello, ma'am."

Mrs. McCray stared vaguely past him to the Cotwells. She looked the wealthy couple up and down, then locked eyes with Laraine. Ilene saw a person straight out of the TV set, one of those evening soap operas where beautiful people wore beautiful clothes and glamorous makeup and had every hair perfectly in place. Ilene stroked her own hair self-consciously and tried to remember if she'd had time to brush it that morning.

Mrs. Cotwell looked around the shabby apartment nervously. Until now, Laraine's idea of a bad apartment was one suffering from the effects of an unfashionable decorator. Of course, Laraine knew there were poor people. She read newspapers. She had been to countless fund raisers, and even organized a few herself.

But, Laraine discovered as she looked into Mrs. McCray's weary eyes, poverty was more than a word. Poverty was people. People who lived in places like this. Children. Children like Baby Bink.

Laraine looked away when one of the agents called from the bedroom. "Sir? In here."

Laraine rushed ahead of Agent Grissom, then shouldered her way past the agent at the bedroom door. Inside the dim room, two children lay on a stained, lumpy mattress on the floor. Their backs were to her, but by their size and clothes, Laraine judged one to be a girl of about two, the other a baby boy about Bink's age.

Hope stirred among the pieces of Laraine's broken heart. *Please, let it be Bink!* Laraine prayed.

She moved slowly to the bed. The thought of holding Bink in her arms made the corners of Laraine's mouth lift in a wobbly smile.

Finally, she reached the mattress and knelt down to see the baby's face. Round, blue eyes opened groggily and stared at Laraine. Hope blurred her vision. For a moment, she felt certain she was looking at Bink. It just had to be him!

But as the baby looked at her, the terrible truth dawned. No. This was not Bink. The adorable bundle looked an awful lot like Laraine's son. But he was not.

Laraine's smile faded. If it was possible to feel worse than she had already, Laraine did. Now that hope's brief candle had been extinguished, the situation seemed even darker.

Small, chubby fingers reached out toward Laraine, like Bink's restless fingers always eager to explore the world. Laraine tenderly stroked the baby's soft hand with her thumb. She gently kissed the smooth skin of his dirty forehead.

Laraine almost didn't want to leave the wretched bedroom where at least she had felt the flicker of hope. She wanted to stay and wash the baby's forehead, hold him on her lap, and read him a story. But she knew that was foolish. Moving with the weariness of a much older woman, Laraine slowly rose and left the room with her husband.

"Sorry if we inconvenienced you," Agent Grissom told Mrs. McCray.

Ilene turned her attention to Laraine. "Is the missing child yours?"

Laraine nodded.

Ilene felt embarrassed. Not knowing how to comfort a stranger suffering such a tragedy, she looked down at the newborn balanced in her arms. What had seemed a few moments ago like a burden, now felt like a blessing.

"I'm sorry," Ilene said softly.

Laraine was surprised by the woman's genuine sympathy for her plight. Here she was living in poverty with more mouths than she could possibly feed, and yet she felt sorry for Laraine.

"You have a beautiful little boy," Laraine managed to say around the lump in her throat.

"Thank you, ma'am," Ilene replied. "I pray yours comes back to you. These kids are all I got, so I know how bad I'd feel if I was in your place."

A sad smile played across Laraine's pretty features. "I hope you never are. For your children's sake."

Then Laraine left the apartment, not wanting the woman to see her cry. The agents followed Laraine, but Bing lingered. Agent Grissom looked at him, with curiosity.

"I'll be there in a second," Bing said.

Grissom stepped out of the apartment and shut the door behind him. Bing reached into the pocket of his hand-tailored English suit. He slipped a thick roll of bills into Ilene's palm. "Sorry for the trouble," Bing explained.

Ilene felt embarrassed again. She wasn't a beggar. She would have given the money back, except that it would help feed her children. And she sensed that the rich man needed to do something at this desperate time, and giving money was all he could do for now.

Bing had already turned to go when she called after him. "Sir? I believe in my heart someone, somewhere watches over the babies."

Bing saw the light of faith in the woman's eyes. He wished he could share her sense of conviction.

"I hope so," he said, then he walked out the door.

chapter 8

*A*s Bing wondered who might be watching over his son, Baby Bink's cab stopped at a curb across the street from the city zoo. The driver hopped out and opened the door for the woman with the many bundles.

While the woman struggled with her packages, Baby Bink crawled out of the cab. He looked across the street and gurgled with joy. Bink saw the zoo, just like in his boo-boo!

The woman paid the driver, but before he could get back in his cab, Eddie, Norby, and Veeko approached him.

"Excuse me . . ." Eddie began.

Veeko opened the cab door and peered inside. The driver stiffened. He didn't know what these three toughs were up to, but he was pretty sure it had to be no good.

Just then, Norby glanced across the street. His eyes bulged. His tongue failed him. For a moment all he could do was point. Then he finally exclaimed, "Eddie!"

Eddie turned and saw Bink crawling across the busy street. The vehicles whizzed by close enough to leave Bink's blond hair blowing in their wake. Baby Bink didn't mind. He was having a great adventure, just like Baby Boo.

Eddie felt the blood pounding in his ears as he watched his retirement fund crawling between the speeding vehicles. This kid was going to give him a heart attack! *How could he . . . What was he . . . ?*

Eddie ran into the street, with Veeko and Norby at his heels. Horns honked. Drivers shook their fists and cursed. But Eddie didn't care.

Then Eddie saw a sight that made his blood run cold. A huge truck was rumbling straight for Baby Bink. Eddie winced and closed his eyes for a second.

His retirement money. Gone. His brilliant Plan. History. Over. Nothing.

Eddie opened his eyes, expecting to see something terrible. But instead, there was Baby Bink! The truck cab had passed right over him. Somehow the child had chosen exactly the right moment to crawl. Miraculously he passed unharmed between the truck-cab tires and the trailer tires.

Eddie was stunned. It just couldn't be! There was no logical explanation for it. And yet, if Eddie had asked Mrs. McCray she would have told him: someone, somewhere watches over the babies.

As it was, Eddie, Norby, Veeko, and the taxi driver watched in amazement as the baby crawled safely to the opposite side of the street. The driver didn't know where the baby had come from. He certainly had no idea Baby Bink had been his passenger moments before. But he did know a baby didn't belong all alone in traffic. So he called his dispatcher.

At first, the taxi driver's boss thought the man was joking. But the dispatcher quickly realized the driver was serious, so he called the police.

While the police operator was asking the dispatcher whether he was joking, Eddie, Veeko, and Norby waited for a clear space in the traffic that poured like a river overflowing in two directions.

When they saw their opportunity, the thieves bolted across the busy street and leaped into a curbside hedge. Eddie, Veeko, and Norby quickly discovered there was a deep, muddy ditch on the other side of the hedge. Ow!

Eddie could not believe what a lousy day he was having. His suit was a wreck. He wondered how long his bruises would take to heal. It seemed like they never would.

Then Eddie remembered the bodybuilders' expression: *No pain, no gain. The Plan was worth it,* he reminded himself. *It had to be!*

Eddie, Norby, and Veeko stumbled into the zoo looking like something scraped off the bottom of a shoe.

Veeko complained, "I worked at Burger King for three years. That was better than this."

Eddie's temper flared. "Don't blame me." He pointed at Norby. "We'd be resting easy if butterfingers here hadn't lost the kid."

Norby shrieked. He couldn't believe Eddie was being so unfair. "I lost the kid? Well, this is news to me."

"Who put himself to sleep reading a nursery story?" Eddie demanded.

Norby felt ashamed, but not enough to take all the blame. "Who left the window open?" he countered.

Veeko hated admitting he'd made a mistake. But he finally confessed, "That was me."

Eddie's eyes searched the curving paths that led around the zoo. The kid had to be somewhere nearby. How fast could he crawl?

While he scanned the groups of schoolchildren, teachers, and food vendors, Eddie griped. "You two are the reason we don't have the kid. As far as I'm concerned, you can drop out now and I'll keep the five million for myself. Frankly, you don't deserve a penny of it."

Veeko was stunned. His itchy hands clenched into furious fists. "You'd stiff us?"

Norby knew they'd never find the kid if they started fighting. "Don't get hot, Eddie. We're just tired of getting all tore apart."

"Like I like to fall off buildings and jump in ditches?" Eddie said. "That's the breaks. We're dealing with a baby. Babies are obviously more dangerous than we thought."

Norby couldn't understand why. "It don't figure. They're so small."

"When I boxed, the guys I most feared were the ones who feared nothing," Eddie recalled. "Babies are like that. They ain't afraid of nothing."

Just then, Eddie spotted something in the soft dirt of the path. Ten little dots, two small palm prints, and two long ruts.

"Baby tracks!" he exclaimed. The kid had crawled this way. Eddie's jaw set with determination. This fight wasn't over yet!

Eddie, Veeko, and Norby followed a trail of baby tracks across the zoo and into the ape house. The summer sun was filtered through skylights inside the yellow brick building. Hairy creatures peered through blue steel bars at the crooks.

Eddie shuddered. The bars reminded him of prison. He hated prison.

Eddie tried to keep his spirits up. The kid had to be here somewhere — and they'd find him!

Eddie, Veeko, and Norby walked past the gorilla cage. Eddie glanced into the enclosure. The back wall of the cage was a panoramic painting of a jungle. The huge, hairy occupant was eating a banana. The ape's cold stare reminded Eddie of his first boxing trainer. But the gorilla wasn't alone.

Eddie, Veeko, and Norby all stopped at the same

time. They walked back to the gorilla cage. They stood at the safety railing staring in disbelief.

Baby Bink was in the ape house all right. He was in the gorilla's cage, sharing the animal's lunch!

A scream shook the building as Eddie, Norby, and Veeko emptied their lungs in utter horror. Schoolchildren leaving the ape house turned to stare at the three screaming men.

Realizing they were being watched, the three criminals quickly turned their screaming into laughter. They nervously waved to the children and the suspicious teacher.

Once the children were gone, Eddie grabbed Norby by the collar and roared, "The kid's in the gorilla cage!"

Veeko shook his head. "Jeez."

Norby was at a loss. "That's it for the five million, huh?"

Eddie looked from the cage to Norby and back again. Norby knew that look. It meant Eddie was about to make him do something dangerous. Norby shook his head. No way was he reaching in that cage to grab the little guy.

Eddie turned his gaze to Veeko, who was watching the gorilla and Baby Bink.

"I think that ape likes the kid," Veeko observed. Then he saw Eddie looking at him. "What?" Veeko asked.

"You got long arms?" Eddie demanded.

Veeko was confused. Then he got worried. Eddie couldn't mean . . . He wouldn't make . . . Veeko looked to Norby for support, but his friend glanced away.

Eddie and Norby stood on either side of the gorilla cage, making sure no zoo visitors would see what Veeko was doing. Inside, the gorilla quietly munched on a slice of apple, but his intelligent, brown eyes never left the hairless apes just beyond the bars.

For the moment, no other visitors were in the ape house. Now was their chance!

Veeko stepped over the safety railing. He eased his arm between the blue bars of the cage. The bars stopped him at the shoulder, but Veeko pressed against them and stretched his fingers toward Baby Bink.

His sweating face was mashed against the cold metal bars. Veeko's fingertips brushed against one of Bink's white shoelaces. He gave it a gentle tug, and Baby Bink started moving slowly toward the bars!

Veeko gritted his teeth and pressed harder against the cage and prepared to pull again. But inside, the gorilla casually gripped Bink's other shoelace between leathery black fingers.

Baby Bink slid back toward the gentle giant. Veeko gave his shoelace a harder tug. The gorilla stared at Veeko.

The thug smiled politely. That had sometimes worked back in school when a teacher had caught him doing something bad.

The gorilla let go of the shoelace! Veeko sighed, then started pulling again. Bink slid toward him.

The gorilla stood up on his powerful legs, and his massive shoulders rolled as he lumbered toward the bars. He sat down again close to Veeko.

Veeko stared at the heavy, brooding brow and scowling muzzle that seemed sculpted out of tough leather. Veeko smiled wider. Charm, that was the answer to this problem, Veeko decided. Charm and shoelaces.

But before he could give the lace another tug, the gorilla suddenly slammed his heavy fist down on Veeko's hand. Pain shot through the thug like a jolt of electricity. Veeko threw back his head and howled.

The gorilla lumbered away from the bars, back to his lunch. Veeko fell to his knees, clutching his smashed hand. For the first time since he'd found the keys, Veeko forgot all about his poison ivy. This was worse!

Eddie and Norby watched their partner kneeling in pain. Then Eddie looked at Norby. Eddie jerked his head back toward the cage. Norby shook his head, no. He felt like he had back in gym class when the coach insisted he join in the football skirmish.

Norby knew he was going to get creamed. But what choice did he have? If the gorilla didn't beat him for trying to get the baby, Eddie would beat him for *not* getting the baby. Norby had once seen Eddie in the boxing ring. He decided his chances were better with the overgrown chimp than with the one-time champ.

Thinking fast, Norby rummaged through a nearby maintenance closet. He found a mop. Norby slid the long handle into the gorilla cage and slipped it under the strap of Baby Bink's overalls. He straddled the mop and bent down. The handle gently lifted Bink off the cage floor.

This is brilliant! Norby thought. *Maybe I can take over as leader after Eddie retires.*

Norby slowly backed away from the cage with the mop balanced between his thighs. As Norby walked, the baby floated closer to the metal bars.

Bink did not like being lifted by the overall straps. He was used to Gilbertine picking him up carefully under the arms. No, no! Baby Bink didn't like this ride at all. He opened his little mouth and cried.

Bink's friend, the big ape, gave an angry snort. He lifted the overall straps off the mop handle and gently set Bink back on the cage floor.

Norby felt frustrated. Here he'd had his first brilliant plan, and this big ape had ruined it! Norby put his hands on his hips in frustration, the way his mother always had when she gave him a good scolding. Norby was too disappointed to bother removing the mop from between his legs.

Suddenly the gorilla leaped into the air. For one horrified second, Norby realized where the creature was headed. But it was too late!

Five hundred pounds of angry ape landed on the mop handle. The other end of the mop slammed into

Norby and sent him flying through the air.

When Norby hit the floor, he decided he didn't care about being leader of the gang. He didn't want to have any more brilliant ideas if they were going to end up like this. All he wanted was for the pain to stop.

Which was exactly what Gilbertine the nanny was thinking at just that moment. Her heart ached as if it always would. Through a haze of tears, Gilbertine stared out the nursery window wondering if she would ever see Bink again.

Gilbertine suddenly realized she wasn't alone. She looked up and saw Mrs. Cotwell standing in the doorway. Laraine crossed the room to sit on the window seat beside Gilbertine.

The nanny struggled to control her sniffles. She didn't want to add to Mrs. Cotwell's distress. "I'm sorry, ma'am."

"I haven't forgotten your feelings," Laraine said to her gently.

"My feelings don't matter," Gilbertine replied, trying to sound brave.

Laraine shook her head. "They do very much." The rich, young woman had been doing a great deal of thinking during this dreadful time. She hoped she could share some of her thoughts with Gilbertine who, up until this terrible day, Laraine had simply regarded as the nice young woman who takes care of Baby Bink.

Gilbertine was surprised by Mrs. Cotwell's remark. She looked at her employer shyly as the woman continued to speak.

"The love my baby has gotten has been as much yours as mine. Probably more," Laraine said ruefully.

For a moment, the two women sat in companionable silence, staring out at the estate's rolling green lawn.

"Where is my little baby?" Laraine wondered. "What's he doing?"

Gilbertine consulted her watch. "If he were home, he'd be going down for his nap."

And that's exactly what Bink was doing. But instead of being snuggled up with his teddy bear in his cozy crib, Bink was curled up against the soft fur of his new friend. The big ape reminded Bink of Curious George. Baby Bink liked his new friend. He was warm and cuddly, like a teddy bear.

Eddie looked at his partners on a nearby bench. Norby was hunched over in pain. Veeko's vacant stare held the same look. His smashed hand was tucked under his arm.

Silently, Eddie pointed to the cage. Then he put his hands to his cheek. The gorilla was asleep. Now was their chance!

Norby and Veeko looked at each other, then at Eddie. He could try if he wanted. They were whipped.

Eddie sighed. Crooks these days had no ambition, no stamina. What was the world coming to? *Obviously,*

Eddie thought, *the only way to get something done right is to do it myself.*

Eddie stepped over the railing and up to the cage. He could hear the gorilla's slow, steady breathing, almost like a snore. *This was going to be as easy as taking candy from a baby, or was that a baby from . . . never mind.*

Eddie reached both arms into the cage and grabbed Bink's ankles. The kid slid to the front of the bars. Now all Eddie had to do was . . .

The lonely gorilla had suspected as much. First, the small furless apes had taken him from the jungle. They had tossed him from one cramped prison to another.

But today one of their young had wandered into his cage, and to his surprise the gorilla had found the infant sweet and gentle. Being with him was like being back home among the trees with his younger brothers and sisters.

And now the adult furless ones wanted to take the infant away. The gorilla had already shaken off two of them. The creatures were cunning, but weak.

The gorilla had suspected the third furless ape would try to take the infant too. He had waited quietly, pretending to sleep. When he felt the infant move, the gorilla lifted one eyelid, just enough to watch the furless adult. While the creature was dragging the infant toward the hard bars, the gorilla reached toward him with his agile toes.

Eddie suddenly felt a firm grip on his arm. Oh, no! The gorilla had his feet around Eddie's wrists.

Eddie's face met the cage bars. Actually, they didn't just meet, they were suddenly married in a touching ceremony in which both partners dissolved their identity completely in union.

Eddie's feet left the ground as enormously strong arms lifted him. Eyes bulging in terror, Eddie saw the gorilla's big, leathery face come closer and closer. Huge jaws ringed with massive teeth gaped open to enclose Eddie's face in a humid cavern that reeked of bananas.

Eddie braced himself for the horror to come. *King Kong is going to eat my face! This is it!*

Eddie felt the gorilla's giant chest swell as he took a deep breath. Then his ears were filled with a roar, low at first, then rising in force and volume until Eddie's face was blown out of the gorilla's mouth. Eddie's wet head snapped back from the tremendous rush of warm, banana-scented air. His ears rang before settling into painful deafness.

Eddie felt the grip on his wrists quickly change. He realized the beast had let go of his feet and now held his hands. Why? What was he going to do next?

Eddie saw Norby and Veeko stand and come closer. They looked scared. Norby's lips formed the word, "Eddie?"

Norby didn't like seeing his boss looking helpless. It kind of shook a guy's faith. If Eddie couldn't handle things, how could Norby hope to get by?

Eddie couldn't answer. The floor was suddenly far away. *No*, Eddie realized. The gorilla had lifted him to the top of the cage. For a moment, the beast just held Eddie suspended at the top of the bars. Then with a powerful thrust of his mighty arms, the gorilla threw Eddie like a football.

Eddie's best dreams had always been about flying, to soar above the clouds, fast and free. But not like this — he was heading straight for the glass ape-house doors.

Relief flooded through him as Eddie heard the automatic doors do their thing. Maybe he wasn't going to die after all. Then a terrible truth occurred to him. What goes up must come down!

While Eddie demonstrated the laws of physics, the gorilla lumbered out of his cage into the afternoon sun. Baby Bink followed him into the outdoor gorilla enclosure.

Bink felt refreshed after his nap. He wanted to explore! Baby Bink waved bye-bye to his big, furry friend. Then he squeezed through a space beneath the bars.

Baby Bink was having a great adventure! He had been on a bus, in a taxi, at the big store, and to the zoo.

Bink crawled along wondering what exciting thing would happen next now that he was having his own day out, just like Baby Boo.

chapter 9

For the second time that day, Norby and Veeko helped their boss to his feet. Knowing that if he wasn't brain-dead Eddie would ask where the baby was, they looked into the gorilla cage. The baby was nowhere in sight!

Eddie watched the ape house and his partners twirl around with shooting stars and meteors. He was dimly aware of Norby and Veeko holding him up.

Eddie struggled to focus his eyes on Norby's face. He dimly heard the young man's voice. "Eddie? I know you don't want to hear this, but the kid's gone again."

Gone, Eddie thought miserably. *Gone again.*

At that moment, Eddie's retirement was crawling through the zoo's park. Bink saw mommies and daddies playing with their children. But he did not see his mommy or his daddy, or his nanny Gilbertine.

Bink's overalls were covered in dirt. His little palms felt gritty. He was tired. And for the first time in his life, there was no one to gently lift him into a warm bath or to tuck him into his soft crib.

Bink watched a mommy wheel her baby in a stroller. He thought of his stroller at home. *Whee!* Bink liked to ride in his stroller.

The mommy saw Baby Bink. She stopped and smiled. "Where's your mommy?" she asked.

Bink crawled away. His mouth puffed in a pout.

The woman watched the baby go. She hoped he would find his mother soon. As she walked away, the woman remarked to her child, "He wasn't a very happy little boy."

Bink's mommy wasn't happy, either. Laraine sat in the library — the last place she had seen Baby Bink. She looked out the window, not seeing anything through her tears. A newspaper was clutched to her chest. Bing sat on the couch nearby. Both were tired with worry and waiting.

Laraine crossed the room to join her husband. Her mind had been churning and churning over the same thoughts. She wanted to share them with Bing. "All the best things about having a child, we paid others to do for us."

Bing bowed his head. It was true. He was glad to know his wife felt the same way.

"Others supplied the time, the concern, and the work. All we wanted was the pride," Laraine continued. "I'm not superstitious or mystical. But somehow, I think this happened to Bink because of us."

Bing couldn't bear to accept that burden. "There's nothing mystical about a criminal taking a child from a wealthy family."

Laraine sighed. Nothing Bing or anyone else said could shake her conviction. "This morning all I wanted was Bink's picture in the paper."

Laraine unfolded the newspaper she'd been holding. Baby Bink's sweet face smiled at her from beneath the bold, front page headline: COTWELL BABY KID-NAPPED!

"I got my wish," Laraine said. Her voice echoed emptily among the scattered shards of her world.

While his mother brooded over her wish, Baby Bink crawled wearily across a wide meadow. The crooks' rusty old van rumbled down the road that divided that meadow. Norby hung out of the passenger window. Eddie hung out of the driver's side. Veeko stared out the front.

"Maybe he went down a rabbit hole," Veeko suggested. He vaguely remembered a children's story with that plot. *Alice in Disneyland* — or something like that.

Eddie snapped, "We're serious about our work. You want to make jokes, join the circus."

Norby was glad Eddie was yelling at Veeko. It meant

the boss wasn't yelling at him. This whole baby thing had made Eddie so cranky!

Norby squinted. Had he seen something crawling through the grass? Norby stared harder. There was something striped like the little guy's shirt moving slowly through the green plants. Norby grinned. The boss would be pleased with him, and maybe he'd get his share of that money after all!

"Step on it, Eddie. Baby off the starboard side," cried Norby.

Bink crawled toward the low cement wall just as the van approached the embankment. The van screeched to a halt. Bink felt scared.

Eddie opened his door and leaned out of the van. Suddenly, his face was all the baby could see. "Did Baby Bink miss his Uncle Eddie?"

Bink did not like the funny men anymore. He was tired of playing with them. He wanted his mommy and daddy, and his nanny Gilbertine.

Bink turned around and scrambled back to the meadow. Eddie jumped out of the van and leaped over the embankment.

"Where'd he go?" Norby asked.

Eddie felt slapped by the impossible again. "He went down a rabbit hole."

Baby Bink crawled through the narrow tunnel. It was like playing in the sandbox, only better! And the big, funny men couldn't follow Bink in here.

Eddie knelt on all fours and peered into the hole. It

reminded him unpleasantly of the gorilla's gaping jaws.

Veeko didn't know much about animals, except that some of them would eat people if you gave them half a chance. "Careful the rabbits don't gnaw up your face, Ed," Veeko cautioned.

Eddie's voice sounded muffled. "Shut, up, Veeko. Just shut up."

Then Eddie saw a light at the end of the tunnel. It was just like the corny posters said. There was a light after all.

Eddie pulled his head out of the hole. "No problem, fellas. It ain't a hole. It's a tunnel. And what's every tunnel got?"

Veeko hated it when people asked questions they already knew the answer to. It reminded him of school. And Veeko had never done well in school. But Eddie was waiting for an answer, so Veeko guessed, "A tollbooth at the end."

Eddie grimaced. "Are you always this stupid, or do you do it just to annoy me? A tunnel's got two ends, and this one's here and the other one's . . ."

By the time Bink reached the other end of the tunnel, the funny men were waiting for him. They grabbed him as soon as he poked his head out of the hole.

"This just ain't your lucky day, short-pants," Norby cackled.

"What's this?" asked Officer LaMarr.

His partner, Peterson, stopped their squad car at the

curb. "Why would anyone leave an empty van here?"

LaMarr shrugged. The old rust bucket's engine was still running. "Let's find out."

The two police officers left their patrol car to get a closer look at the abandoned vehicle.

At that moment, Eddie, Veeko, and Norby emerged from the woods. Norby laughed. Things were finally going their way. He had the little guy square around the waist. No way was the kid getting away now!

Suddenly, Eddie stopped walking. Norby followed the direction of Eddie's gaze and saw the police officers looking at the van.

Norby shoved the kid into Veeko's arms. Veeko thrust the tyke into Eddie's. Veeko remembered playing hot potato when he was a boy — and he had no intention of getting stuck holding this hot potato when the heat came down.

When Officers LaMarr and Peterson spotted the three men, they were seated on a nearby park bench. The man in the middle had his jacket over his lap.

Eddie prayed the kid would stay quietly under the jacket until he could get rid of the law.

"Beautiful day, huh?" Eddie said casually. He slid his hand over Baby Bink's mouth as the cops approached.

"You know anything about this vehicle?" Officer LaMarr demanded.

Eddie adopted his good-citizen voice. "Yes, sir. It belongs to us."

"You left the engine running," LaMarr said. The man

looked nervous. The police officer wondered why.

Bink explored the dark world beneath the jacket. His little fingers reached between Eddie's legs and squeezed.

Eddie jumped with a sudden surge of pain, which he struggled to hide from the cop's suspicious gaze.

"Yiii-es. I did," Eddie managed to say. *Yow!*

"I've been having batterrrrrry, troublllle," Eddie fibbed. "We just stopped to — ow! — admire the beautiful FLOWERS!"

Finally, the squeezing stopped. Eddie sighed with relief.

"Have you seen a baby around here?" Officer LaMarr asked. The whole force was turning the city upside down trying to find the Cotwell kid. If LaMarr found him, it would mean a promotion. He sure could use a raise.

Eddie felt the restless little hands reach into his pocket and pull out his cigarette lighter. What was the kid up to now? Wasn't it bad enough the law was nosing around with a bunch of questions?

"The park is full of babies," Eddie said. *Just stay cool!* he told himself. Then he heard the sound of his lighter being struck.

"There's been a kidnapping," Officer Peterson explained in the stiff way cops talked.

"That's a shame," Norby said with exaggerated sincerity. "Boy, what some people won't do for money."

"For five million," Veeko added.

103

Eddie glared at him. How could he stay cool when his partner was about to reveal their involvement? Then Eddie realized there was another reason he wasn't staying as cool as he'd hoped. That brat had left the lighter on — Eddie's pants were on fire! The heat was starting to spread from the loose fabric to his legs. They had to get rid of the cops now!

"If we see anything . . ." Eddie began. He closed his knees around Baby Bink's middle. He had to hold the kid in place or their goose was cooked. And that's not all that was cooking.

Baby Bink let out a big belch. It felt good! Nanny Gilbertine usually burped him after lunch.

Eddie covered his mouth, hoping the cops would think he'd made the noise.

"Excuse me," Eddie said hastily. The fire was growing! "If we see anything, we'll notify — Jeez! Oh! Holy Heaven! Excuse me — the police. Thank you."

Eddie stretched his arm up on the bench in what he hoped looked like a casual gesture. He was really trying to bring his mouth closer to Norby's ear. Eddie whispered, "Walk 'em to the car!"

Norby slapped his knee and started to rise. "We better get going. We can't leave our vehicle in the roadway."

Officer LaMarr looked back at the van. From this distance he spotted the familiar features, instead of just the rust. "Is that a Fleetline van?" he asked.

Eddie struggled to keep from screaming. *Would these*

cops never leave? "Yeah."

LaMarr smiled. He liked being right. "I thought so. My brother drives one of them for a dry-cleaning outfit."

Eddie said, "Good."

LaMarr remembered his brother complaining about his van. "I know he's had a lot of trouble with his. Give me a second and I'll think of what he said is wrong with the electrical system."

Eddie squirmed. A helpful cop. Just what he needed while his pants burned to cinders.

"Alternator?" suggested Officer Peterson.

LaMarr looked thoughtful for a moment, then shook his head. "No."

"There's a little relay thing," Veeko prompted. He loved cars. They were among the few things Veeko knew anything about.

LaMarr brightened. "That sounds familiar."

"What's it called . . . Darn. I'll think of it," Veeko began. Then he saw Eddie's panicked expression.

"VEEKO! Veeko? I think you better move THE VAN," Eddie said. Realizing his voice sounded funny, he added, "I got a frog in my throat."

Eddie leaned over to Norby again and whispered fiercely, "And a brush fire in my shorts. Get 'em outta here!"

Norby stood up quickly. "It's just a bad battery, and we better move it before it dies."

Norby eased the cops to the roadway. Officer

Peterson inhaled deeply. Suddenly he felt hungry. "You can sure tell summer's here. People have those barbecues going."

While Norby, Veeko, and the police officers walked to the van, Eddie stayed on the bench.

"I'll be there in a minute. I have a cramp in my LEG!" he called after them. Tears rolled down Eddie's cheeks. This kid was going to be the death of him!

Eddie felt the kid squirm away. The thief was in too much pain to stop him. There'd be time enough to deal with the kid once the cops were on their way and the fire was put out.

Bink slipped under the bench and crawled into the woods. Eddie watched him go, marking the direction and muttering under his breath, "You ain't never gonna see your folks again!"

Eddie waved casually to the departing cops. Once the squad car was out of sight, the scream that had been building in Eddie's throat escaped in full-fledged fury. He tore the coat off his lap. The burst of fresh air turned the smoldering fire into flames shooting up from his pants.

Veeko and Norby stared at their leader in horror. Too panicked to think clearly, Eddie jumped up and down, dancing around like a lunatic under a full moon. His flailing attempts to extinguish the blaze only fed it further.

Veeko and Norby raced to the rescue. They grabbed Eddie's arms and threw him on his back. Veeko lifted his leg, then brought it down hard on Eddie. Veeko stamped and stomped until the fire was completely out.

"Eddie? You okay?" Norby asked.

Eddie struggled to his knees. His dark eyes bored two holes of pure hate through Veeko.

"That's what you do with campfires," Veeko said.

Eddie panted. "Is that a fact?"

"I used to do it in the Boy Scouts," Veeko said proudly.

Eddie was so angry, he couldn't control himself. He leaped up, grabbed Veeko, and hurled the young thug into the woods. "Follow that darn kid! We'll meet you on the other side."

Veeko finally realized Eddie didn't think he was a hero. He guessed having your pants stomped might make anyone mad. "I'm sorry, man. It was an emergency. You were blazing pretty darn —"

"Shut up!" Eddie shrieked.

Norby stared at the gaping hole in Eddie's pants. "Boy, you were burned clear through your Skivvies."

Eddie waddled to the van, wincing with each step.

chapter 10

*B*aby Bink heard heavy trucks nearby. He spotted the top of a tall construction crane over a paneled wooden fence. Boo-boo! Bink knew where he was now. He was at a building site, just like the one Baby Boo saw on his day out.

Bink crawled to a wide gap between the boards. He saw stacks of bright orange blocks, much bigger than the ones in his nursery. He saw big strong workers in their yellow hats and blue jeans. They looked just like the workers in his boo-boo! And there were big trucks driving around with loads of dirt, just like in the sandbox at the park.

Bang, bang went their hammers. *Fizz! Fizz!* Bright sparks flew from their welding torches. Baby Bink was entranced.

He sat in the soft dirt between deep tire ruts. Bink

didn't know he was sitting in the truck entrance. Then there was a loud rumbling. A truck loaded with steel passed right over Bink.

When it was gone, Bink crawled away. He wanted to see more of the big sandbox.

Bink crawled toward a worker who was sitting on a steel girder. The man was drinking coffee and eating a doughnut. Bink liked doughnuts!

Baby Bink grinned. He crawled toward the box of doughnuts. Bink didn't notice the giant bucket of cement that smashed down on the place where he'd just been sitting.

The worker didn't notice Bink. The man finished his coffee and went back to work. Bink crawled onto the bright orange girder. There was half a doughnut left in the box. Bink's little fingers seized the doughnut. *Yum, yum!*

Baby Bink sucked on the sweet doughnut. It was so good, he didn't notice when the girder began to rise. Bink didn't notice the funny man, either.

But Veeko had spotted Bink! He ran to meet the van as it chugged out of an alley. Veeko stuck his head in the window and said breathlessly, "I got bad news."

Eddie wondered if he would ever hear any other kind.

Veeko continued, "The kid's in there."

Eddie leaned out the van window and looked where Veeko was pointing. At just that moment, the crane lifted Baby Bink's girder high enough for the crooks to see.

Eddie's jaw dropped in utter horror. *His retirement was riding to its doom!*

Bink thought this was the best ride — even better than the bumpy van and the elevator! He saw the funny men on the street below him. They looked smaller and smaller the higher Bink rode. The men looked very silly as they scrambled into the construction site.

"Get him!" Eddie shrieked. His voice was sore. It had been a very long day. It had, in fact, been the worst day of Eddie's life. And, he realized with a sense of impending disaster, it wasn't over yet.

Bink giggled. The city stretched beneath him in all its busy splendor. There were trucks and yellow taxis, and busy people no bigger than toys scurrying here and there.

Baby Bink watched the miniature-sized Eddie, Norby, and Veeko clamber into the flimsy metal cage of the construction elevator. Eddie slammed the door shut and felt the cage shudder as it started to ascend.

"Eddie?" Veeko said.

Eddie was tired. He was more than tired, but he couldn't let himself think of that. "What?" he asked.

"My butt hurts," Veeko complained.

Eddie stared at his young partner as if Veeko had just spoken in Martian.

"Them van seats are all busted-up. They hurt my butt," Veeko whined.

Eddie's dark eyes stared out of the metal cage. He saw the ground sink beneath his feet. The windows in buildings across the street blurred past his eyes. "We're flying up the side of a building with nothing between us and the earth but chicken wire and you're worried about your sore butt?"

Panic gripped Norby's heart as tightly as the fat lady's arm had circled Veeko's neck. "How come you had to say that about the chicken wire?" Norby demanded.

"How come?" Eddie asked impatiently. "'Cause it's true."

Norby swallowed with difficulty. His mouth felt dry and his head felt dizzy. "I was trying very hard not to think about heights."

"With the wind whistling through your hair at a hundred miles an hour, you're not gonna think about heights? What are you gonna think about — trout fishing?" Eddie wondered.

While Norby struggled to ignore Eddie's comment about the whistling wind, Veeko pointed and exclaimed, "Eddie! Baby at twelve o'clock."

Eddie looked up and saw Bink on his girder. The elevator had almost reached the same level. Baby Bink saw the funny men and waved.

The elevator passed the girder. "We'll be with you in just a minute," Eddie assured the kid through gritted teeth.

They stopped the elevator at the next floor. As the door opened, Veeko teased "Lingerie, home furnishings, men's hats, babies . . ."

He laughed at his own wit, but Eddie and Norby just stepped out of the elevator.

Norby was confused. "Wait a second. We passed him."

"Exactly," Eddie said. "We'll grab him as he goes by."

Called to a higher floor, the elevator moved up. Eddie looked into the empty elevator shaft and saw Bink's girder gliding slowly up to their floor. Eddie put a hand on Veeko's shoulder.

Veeko said, "That's a good plan, Ed. We grab him when he comes by."

"You grab him," Eddie corrected.

"I grab him?" Veeko asked. The plan didn't sound so good when Eddie put it that way.

"Right," Eddie declared. "As the girder comes up, you jump out on it and grab the baby."

"Me? By myself?" Veeko asked.

"You just step out on it," Eddie explained. "It ain't difficult."

Veeko's mind clung to the central idea, just as his feet liked to cling to solid ground. "Why me?"

"Norby's scared of heights," Eddie said.

"Why don't *you* do it?" Veeko asked.

"Nobody asked me," Eddie replied with perfect logic.

Veeko couldn't argue with that. "Oh," he said simply.

Then, as the girder slowly neared the empty shaft, Veeko braced himself for the jump. He sprang into space and grabbed the girder. The beam swung away from the building, out and down.

Bink slid along the smooth orange beam. He thought of the swings in the park. Baby Bink loved going to the park with Nanny Gilbertine. This ride was fun too!

Veeko clung to the other end of the I beam. He heard a familiar noise. Veeko looked up with mounting horror. The noise was the elevator coming back down.

The beam swung again. This time Baby Bink slid onto the roof. He landed on his little hands and knees. He wondered why the funny men looked so mad. Why were they always waving at him and yelling?

Eddie and Norby stared in disbelief.

"How'd he do that?" Norby marveled.

Eddie shrugged. "Baby luck."

Baby luck saw Bink through an amazing series of near-misses and high-altitude hijinks. Unfortunately for Eddie, Norby, and Veeko, the only kind of luck crooks have is bad.

Baby Bink thought the funny men were funnier than they had ever been. They did tricks and screamed and tumbled just like the clowns at the circus. Baby Bink laughed and laughed!

While Baby Bink landed smile-up no matter how many girders he rode, Eddie and his partners slammed, flipped, flopped, tripped, dropped, and banged their way from one disaster to the next.

In the end, Baby Bink landed safely in the construction yard. Norby wound up neck deep in wet cement. An encounter with an out-of-control cart shot Veeko into a dumpster. And, after a long and painful chase, Eddie found himself swinging thirty stories above the ground at the end of a huge steel hook. He clung to the crane with the same fierce desperation that he had clung to The Plan.

It was over. Eddie was finally ready to kiss his dream good-bye. All he wanted now was to get down — in one piece!

The five-o'clock whistle blew, and workers poured out of the yard. Baby Bink crawled out with them.

One tipped his yellow hardhat to scratch his head. "I think I just saw a baby," he remarked.

His buddy looked around and asked, "Where?"

But Bink was gone, like Eddie's hopes. Just in case, the confused worker called the cops.

chapter 11

*T*hat night, Agent Grissom went to the Cotwell mansion to make a report. He found Laraine and Bing curled up on the couch in the library. Gilbertine sat across the room with Sally and Mr. Andrews.

"I have some news," Grissom said by way of greeting. "I don't know if it's good. But it isn't bad."

Laraine felt alive for the first time in hours. Bing also snapped to attention.

"Since the media spread the story, calls are coming in." The agent paused to consult some notes. "There was a report of a man looking for a lost baby on a bus this morning. A baby being taken from a department store care center. Another in City Park at 3:00 P.M. Shortly after that at the zoo."

Gilbertine's slumped shoulders suddenly straightened. This all sounded very familiar to her. *Bus,*

117

department store, park, zoo . . . Gilbertine waited anxiously for Grissom to continue.

"And a final report, not long ago at —"

"A building under construction!" cried Gilbertine triumphantly.

The agent stared at the nanny. His professional suspicion was aroused. *How could she know? Was she somehow involved in the plot?*

"That's right," he said slowly, watching her face for reaction.

"He's doing everything in the book!" Gilbertine explained excitedly. Relief flooded through her like sunshine. "I know where he is!"

Laraine and Bing were shocked. How could Gilbertine know where Bink was when they had no idea?

Grissom flipped to a fresh page on his notepad and listened carefully as Gilbertine closed her eyes, folded her hands in her lap, and recited the familiar text she knew by heart. "Before returning home for supper, Nanny and Baby Boo stopped at the Old Soldiers' Home to visit Mr. Tinsel."

Laraine, Bing, and Agent Grissom stared at Gilbertine in amazement. Had the nanny gone bananas? But she seemed so certain — and they all wanted so badly for Bink to be safe.

Soon FBI and police vehicles along with a black limousine poured out of the Cotwell's long driveway. The whole parade drove at top speed to a home for aged veterans. A flag snapped in the breeze above the old brick building. The brass door handles were worn with age, but lovingly polished.

Laraine and Bing raced into the lobby. The faint sound of singing drifted down a hall. In voices quivering with age, veterans were singing an old World War I song.

"This is the Army, Mr. Jones,
No private rooms or telephones.
You had your breakfast in bed before . . ."

The anxious parents and their police escort followed the sound to the lounge. They froze in the doorway, astonished by the vision that met their eyes. A dozen white-haired veterans were sitting in a circle around Baby Bink!

Could it be? Laraine could hardly believe the nightmare was over. Was he really safe? Was she dreaming?

Laraine's eyes misted at the sight of her beautiful son bouncing on an old-timer's knee. The veterans sang heartily and Bink clapped his little hands.

"This is the Army, Mr. Green,
We like the barracks nice and clean.
You had a housemaid to clean your floor . . ."

Bing felt a surge of love swell his heart. He could not remember ever being so swept up by such an emotion.

119

Bing had always been a stiff-upper-lip sort of man — even as a boy. But now . . .

"This is the Army, Mr. Brown,
You and your baby went to town.
She had you worried . . ."

Laraine saw the old-timer lift Bink over his head as the men finished with a flourish.

"And she won't worry you anymore!"

Bink looked up and saw his mommy and daddy standing in the doorway. They had found him. Bink clapped his hands and grinned. He was tired. He had enjoyed his big adventure. But now he was ready to go home, just like Baby Boo.

The old soldiers followed the direction of Bink's gaze. They watched as Bing and Laraine raced into the room. Laraine scooped Bink up in her arms and held him as if she would never let go.

"Baby!" she cried.

Gilbertine smiled warmly as she watched the reunion of mother and child. Laraine's face was radiant with joy and love.

Laraine's face was still shining as the limo pulled away from the veterans' home. Agent Grissom and Gilbertine sat on the second set of seats facing the happy couple and their child.

Bing leaned in close and told Baby Bink, "You had quite an adventure today."

Baby Bink squirmed around on his mother's lap to look out the limousine's rear window. The setting sun shone brightly on a clock billboard in the distance. Baby Bink knew that sign. It was the same TIME FOR FLAVOR billboard that topped the crooks' building.

Bink pointed excitedly. "Boo-boo! Boo-boo!"

Gilbertine leaned forward to comfort her small charge. She knew he must be distressed by the loss of his favorite book. "Bink? Sweetie? We'll get another boo-boo."

Bing was confused. And now that they had come through this terrible ordeal, Bing was determined to know everything about his young son. "Boo-boo?" he asked.

Gilbertine explained, "That's what he calls his book. He lost it today."

"Boo-boo! Boo-boo! Boo-boo!" Bink cried.

"We'll get another one, Bink," Laraine said, bending to plant yet another kiss on Bink's head.

Baby Bink turned back to face his mommy. He put his little hands on her cheeks and turned her head to the window. Bink wanted Mommy to see what he was seeing. But Mommy turned her head away.

"No, sweetheart," Laraine said. She could not imagine what Bink wanted. Everything she cared about was right there in that car.

But Bink persisted in pointing and trying to get his

mommy's attention. "Boo-boo!" Bink cried again.

Finally, Laraine got the idea. "You want me to look? Okay."

She glanced out the window at the urban landscape. A tacky billboard winked in the orange sun. "I see. That's nice," Laraine said politely.

"Boo-boo!" Baby Bink felt frustrated. Why didn't Mommy understand? "Boo-Boo!" He grabbed her face again and turned her back to the window.

Laraine stared blankly at the billboard. Why did children have to be so confusing? Why couldn't Bink just ask for what he wanted in plain English? Laraine realized she had a lot to learn about child care. She hoped Gilbertine could help her.

"That's not a boo-boo," Laraine said with exaggerated patience. "That's a clock. Tick-tock."

Then she turned to the nanny. "Was there a tick-tock in his book?"

Gilbertine shook her head. "No."

Laraine said, "He's pointing to —"

Something suddenly occurred to her. "His boo-boo!" she said to Agent Grissom intently. "He's not pointing to the tick-tock! He's pointing to his boo-boo! He wants his boo-boo!"

Agent Grissom said, "I thought he was getting a new boo-boo."

"He means his boo-boo's back there!" Laraine exclaimed. It was suddenly clear. "That's where he's been!"

Agent Grissom felt as if a dozen light bulbs had just switched on in his head. He leaned back to address the agent sitting beside the limo driver. "Radio Rogers and McCloskey and tell them we're turning around to go to the tick-tock to get the boo-boo. And send for backup."

Once the driver understood the strange command, the big car swung around in a fast U-turn, then roared down the street. The driver kept the clock billboard in his sight.

Squad cars squealed after the speeding black vehicle. When the limo reached the block with the billboard, it slowed to cruising speed. All eyes were on Baby Bink as he looked out the window.

Suddenly, he pointed. "Boo-boo! Boo-boo! Boo-boo!"

In the apartment below the billboard, Eddie, Veeko, and Norby slumped in front of the flickering television set. Their various lumps, bumps, bruises, cuts, and scratches had been crudely bandaged and smeared with sticky ointments. Many aspirins had been swallowed, but nothing could ease the pain of failure.

The Plan had been a total washout. No, worse than a washout. The Plan had almost been the death of Eddie. Maybe it was time to go back to thinking small.

Norby could not accept that it had all been for nothing. "You don't want to go see if they left the money?"

Eddie sneered. "That's a good idea. We get torn apart by a baby. Three fully grown men versus fifteen pounds of pink flesh with a mouth. What chance you think we got of strolling into that alley and coming out with any less than a hundred and forty years in prison? No thanks. This is a hexed situation. We walk away while we're ahead."

Veeko attempted a joke. "We took a lickin' and we kept on tickin'."

Eddie glared at his dumb partner. But Norby and Veeko were all he had.

"We'll go back to banks," Eddie decided. "Dealing with grownups. I don't want no more kiddie stuff."

"We did good with banks," said Norby, ever the optimist.

"And every now and then a convenience store," Veeko recalled fondly. "To keep things interesting."

"Or a jewelry store," Norby suggested.

Veeko agreed, "Or a jewelry store."

Eddie sighed. They weren't dead. That was something. "I don't want to ever hear another word about that rotten, snakebit baby," he said. And then he heard a faint "Boo-boo! Boo-boo!" in the distance.

Eddie thought his mind was playing tricks on him. Maybe it was his long-forgotten conscience that had woken up and decided to start nagging him, the way consciences were supposed to. Maybe Norby or Veeko were throwing their voices like ventriloquists, or it was some kind of crazy ghost or something. Because Eddie knew one thing: IT COULDN'T BE WHAT HE THOUGHT IT WAS!

"Boo-boo! Boo-boo!" Eddie heard the voice again, this

time more clearly. But Veeko and Norby just stared blankly, making too much of their own noise to hear the strange voice.

"I'm serious," Eddie barked. "I'm hearing that kid in my thoughts. I want to erase him from my mind."

"Boo-boo! Boo-boo! Boo-boo!"

There it was again. Eddie remembered some horror movie he'd been to once where the guy who killed some other guy and bricked him up in the wall kept hearing the dead guy screaming to get out. Eddie shuddered.

Veeko and Norby were finally quiet. Norby looked at Eddie. Eddie looked at Veeko. No, he wasn't going crazy. They heard it too. But how?

"You hear that?" Norby asked.

"Yeah," Veeko grunted.

"You know what that sounds like?" Norby demanded.

A terrible thought passed through Eddie's dazed mind. He leaned over. On the floor was that storybook. Eddie picked it up. Evidence. They'd have to ditch it. But there was something more. Something worse.

"Boo-boo," he said softly. Eddie's eyes widened in horror. He knew what the strange phrase meant, and, worse still, he knew that soft voice.

"He's back," the doomed man concluded.

Five flights below, the front door of the shabby tenement was kicked in by a pair of heavy boots. Cops swarmed into the dingy lobby and up the sagging stairs.

The three crooks scrambled to the window, only to see a flock of police sharpshooters scattered on every rooftop, like birds of prey poised to pounce. Helicopters buzzed like angry hornets. Bright lights swept over the quiet street.

Down below, Baby Bink gazed up at Eddie. A big smile lit the child's features. His chubby fingers waved.

Eddie curled his lip and fumed. "You dirty, no good, little narc!"

Baby Bink bounced in his daddy's arms. He put his fingers to his mouth and blew the kidnappers a big kiss.

Eddie flinched at the familiar blare of a bullhorn.

"You're surrounded! Throw down the boo-boo and put your hands over your heads."

Eddie flipped the storybook out the window. He watched it flutter down five stories like a wounded pigeon, like all his shattered dreams. Eddie wondered if he should follow the book. Then he remembered that the fall hadn't killed him the first time. Knowing his luck, it would just add bruises to his bruises.

The book landed on the pavement. Laraine noticed that it was open to the last page. She picked up the book and studied the picture. Then she held it up for Baby Bink to see.

"This is the end of the story," Laraine said.

Baby Bink smiled and pointed to the picture of Baby Boo and his mommy and daddy at home in their house.

Which is where Baby Bink was a little while later, safe and snug in his soft crib. He was clean and dressed in fluffy pajamas, sucking his thumb.

Laraine and Bing stood in the nursery door gazing fondly at their son. Finally, they switched off the light.

"Good night, sweetheart," Laraine said softly. She could not believe this had all happened in only one day. She felt as if she had lived a lifetime since greeting Baby Bink that morning.

"Good night, Bink," Bing echoed. It seemed like he couldn't look at the little fellow long enough. But the baby needed his rest, and they did too. So Bing quietly shut the door.

Alone in his nursery, Bink crawled to the end of his crib and reached over to his bookshelf. His chubby fingers grabbed a book.

Baby Bink's adventure was finally over. Or was it?

By the moon's soft silver glow, Bink feasted his eyes on the cover of the pretty book. The book cover made Bink smile, even though he could not read the words: *Baby's Trip to China.*